JOSHUA S

Gwendoline Riley was born in 1979. Her first
novel, *Cold Water*, won a Betty Trask Award.
Her second, *Sick Notes*, was published in 2004

GWENDOLINE RILEY

Joshua Spassky

VINTAGE BOOKS
London

Published by Vintage 2008

2 4 6 8 10 9 7 5 3

Copyright © Gwendoline Riley 2007

Gwendoline Riley has asserted her right under the Copyright, Designs
and Patents Act 1988 to be identified as the author of this work

First published in Great Britain by Jonathan Cape in 2007

Vintage
Random House, 20 Vauxhall Bridge Road,
London SW1V 2SA

www.vintage-books.co.uk

Addresses for companies within The Random House Group Limited can be
found at: www.randomhouse.co.uk/offices.htm

The Random House Group Limited Reg. No. 954009

A CIP catalogue record for this book
is available from the British Library

ISBN 9780099490692

Penguin Random House is committed to a sustainable future for
our business, our readers and our planet. This book is made from
Forest Stewardship Council® certified paper.

Printed and bound in Great Britain by Clays Ltd, St Ives plc

For Jimmy Jimmereeno

'Karamazov!' Kolya cried, 'Is it really true what religion says, that we shall all rise up from the dead and come to life and see one another again, and everyone, even Ilyushechka?'

'Without question we shall rise, without question we shall see one another, and joyfully tell one another everything that has happened,' half laughing, half in ecstasy, Alyosha replied.

The Brothers Karamazov, Fyodor Dostoyevsky

1

Jeane came to see me before I left.

'Come in,' I said. 'Come on in. It's like the set of Beckett's something or other in here.'

She followed me down the hallway. In the dark kitchen, she opened the empty fridge – I saw her placid face lit up – and shut it again. In the empty living room she paced slowly around, her hands in her raincoat pockets. I sat back down on the floor.

After she'd joined me, I flicked a dust ball towards her. A tiny cloud of bent hair knots and grey fluff. It floated along.

'So, anyway,' I said, 'I have this image in my mind, of a pig with its throat cut, and with all of its legs still twitching. I'm crossing the ocean. Is that just a spasm?'

Jeane frowned. After a moment she took in a breath and huffed it out.

'I'm not sure,' she said.

And then: 'You know, Mick still phones me

every now and then. To say he still loves me and to check I still love him. He says, "I know circumstances are tough, they're tough for me too, I'm just phoning to *check*." It's funny. It's fine. Whether we're together or not is a piece of trivia. I don't think love is a matter of logistics, Natalie. Love is there,' she said, and she looked at me as she patted her hand on the floor.

'It's right there.' She patted the same place, rubbed the orange laminate. 'All the time. Like a – saucer.'

'So why press the point?' I said. 'Good question. Maybe I'm going in order to mock God.'

'Oh, really.'

I stood up and brushed off my itchy hands, walked over to the cold window.

'If you think I'm throwing my life up for the sake of rhetorical excitement then you're only half-right. But then again, what else is there? Maybe there isn't much else.'

'Maybe,' she said. 'Speaking of which, all I ate yesterday was half a cabbage, shredded. I thought that might be funny, but it's just been upsetting.'

I could see her grinning to herself behind me, pushing her hair back out of her face.

'You're turning into the Dalai Lama,' I said,

peering down, now, at the cobbled alley behind my building.

My old settee was still there. Filthy and slouched. I'd dragged it outside late one night last week, and now it was making me feel guilty. I kept waiting for it to be taken – by whatever mysterious agencies take waterlogged settees from city streets.

'Just so long as I don't have to be fucking re-incarnated,' Jeane said.

'Sorry?'

'Are you coming back?' she said.

2

I'd thrown nearly everything away. Now there was this: an old letter from Bompa Bramwell to my Grandma:

> 16, Oakwood Drive, Driffield
> 9th January '58

My Dear Hilda,

Don't upset yourself too much by what I am going to tell you but the Home Help found Auntie had passed away during the night of yesterday the 8th. It was best it happened that way. The Home Help said she looked very peaceful and had passed in her sleep.

She was ever so cheerful on Tuesday and told Mr. and Mrs. Rime she was going to the Whist Drive with them that night. When she was ready they hadn't arrived to take her so she was on her way on her own when they caught up with her. She won a prize (1/3d) and Uncle Herbert has it in a white purse that she had. (I have been up to Nora's to see him this morning.)

*Mr. and Mrs. Rime went in with Auntie to help
her to get to bed and Auntie took a hot water bottle
up. The Home Help said she found the bed wet
through, though — she hadn't put the stopper in
correctly.*

*The funeral is at 11 o'clock at Kemberworth Church
on Saturday. I'll get a spray for you so don't worry.
The Co-op are attending to things. Of course Uncle
Herbert didn't let me know how much insurance
there is. He and Nora have done all the arranging.
Well, all my love and look after yourselves,*
Pa

*P.S. If Jane still hasn't sent that thank you note
well she won't need to bother now.*

No, she won't, I thought — I was sitting on the
bedroom floor with the latest bin bag next to me
— and I tore the thin, dry pages in two. I put them,
and a small stack of others like them, into the bag.

Jane was my Mum, Bompa Bramwell my Great-
Grandad. I met him a couple of times — if met is
the right word. The last time was on a visit to his
rest home with Mum and Grandma, one summer
when I was maybe eight or nine. Our car had
bumped and swerved down the Snake Pass that
morning, crossing the Pennines.

'Concentrate on the middle distance,' Mum said.

But there was no middle distance; there were just steep inclines: boulders and shaggy old rams somehow staying put there. And the car was so hot, Grandma's cologne was so heavy; Mum had to pull over for me. Afterwards she leant back between the seats to rub my mouth with a tissue, to rub my head and tut. She gave me her little brown ammonia bottle, and I sniffed at it curiously for the rest of the way there.

Bompa was one hundred and two then, and still doggedly *compos mentis* if not exactly spry. When we arrived, he was sitting in a straight-backed armchair by his bedroom window; the bright sunlight streaming in making an eerie cosmos of all the dust that floated around him. I was cajoled into standing next to him there, and then Mum and Grandma looked on as he gripped my elbow.

'Thank you for that birthday card,' he said, looking up in my direction, and whistling through a false-teeth smile. 'It was very o*rig*inal.'

The card, dried pasta stuck on sugar paper, was still propped up on his bedside table.

Grandma's older sister, Elsie, received a visit that day, too. She took a long time to answer her doorbell, and then we all followed her back into her bungalow: a slow procession down a long hallway.

'Gosh, it's hot,' Grandma said, pulling at the neck of her blouse.

Before we went through to the parlour, Mum turned to me and whispered, '*Remember to SMILE.*'

She did it herself to demonstrate, baring her teeth and tilting her head.

'So, you'll have seen Pa then,' Elsie said.

And then she and Grandma, having sat down on the cramped little sofa in the window, set to discussing who else was poorly or dead. Mum leant forward in her chair, listening politely, smiling expectantly.

Elsie and Grandma looked very alike. Their profiles, bent together, matched perfectly. It was only that Grandma was made up for her away day – with powder, jammy lipstick, dabs of peachy blusher – whereas Elsie just looked scrubbed, pouchy and thread-veined. They both had thin, fawn-coloured hair. Elsie's, moulting, lay in bristles on the collar of her housecoat.

A framed photograph on the mantelpiece showed them as fat-kneed toddlers in smocks and buckle shoes, standing by a wall and each holding a stick of rhubarb like a pikestaff. Next to that was a head shot of their brother, a moon-faced boy in RAF uniform. Those photos came to our house eventually. I remember Mum saying, 'Isn't it amazing? Poor things.'

After twenty minutes or so, Elsie pulled the clingfilm off the plate of sandwiches she'd made, and we all took one. I kept chewing on my first bite: a mash of dry bread, fish paste, leathery bits of cucumber. I turned it over in my mouth. Mum must have noticed.

'Why don't you go and sit on the patio?' she said. 'Get some fresh air.'

And so, safely out of view, I spat the lump out in a flowerbed, covered it over with gravel and soil. I put what was left of the sandwich under a bush, and spent the rest of the visit out there in the garden, sitting in a cane chair, making eyes at the neighbour's cat.

After we'd dropped Grandma home, Mum told me how Great-Uncle Wilf, the man on the mantelpiece, had died. I'd moved into the front seat then, and I was watching Mum drive and tell the story, about how after he came back from the war, Wilf had taken to drink.

'He became a menace,' Mum said, and I nodded.

'One night he was limping home across the

moors, and he'd been to a spring fête, so he was wearing women's clothes, a dress and a bonnet. He was drunk, and it was stormy, and somehow, he fell in a bog. They didn't find him until the floodwater receded, and as your Grandma tells it, the mud was holding him upright, like a scarecrow.'

'Oh no,' I said, and I tried to picture it.

Mum nodded and flicked on the indicator.

Tick tock tick tock . . .

All this inert apocrypha. 'Memory Lane', in a squashed cardboard box I'd pulled out from under my bed.

I continued to fill the bin bag with these brittle documents, half-scrunched up, or torn into flakes. I put in the first letter Dad sent Mum after she left him. He wrote on mauve notepaper, pleading his case in capital letters:

THE NUMBNESS IS WEARING OFF BUT IT STILL PAINS,

he wrote, and:

MY STOMACH WAS THE FIRST THING TO GO.

and:

JIM SAYS LEAVE IT AND SHE'LL COME
BACK. HAVEN'T TOLD MOTHER YET.

In their wedding pictures they stood together in the registry-office car park. To look at those photos was to imagine Dad putting his suit on that morning, running his comb under the tap. Also it was to imagine him with his foot on Mum's throat – if you were so inclined. And I generally was. There they were anyway: that's what they did thirty years ago. The smudged fingerprints on the celluloid were an oily, neon blue.

Elsewhere in the box, there were some photos of Mum when she was at university: the only woman on the electronics course at Chelsea College. Most of those pictures had a jagged hole cut in them, where she'd nail-scissored out the face of a boyfriend she had there.

But there was all sorts in that box; it wasn't all to do with my dead family. It was just a grocery box I'd marker penned with 'MISC'.

I picked out an airmail envelope next. Leaning back against the bed, I read the first page:

Department of Humanities
Chicago State University

Dear Natalie,
I was doing some research the other day and I found
something that I think is pretty interesting. You know
that when you're taken into police custody, you have
a right to consult your solicitor (or have the state
provide one). In fact, you don't need to use a solic-
itor and can ask to have a friend come in instead.
I'm not aware of anybody actually doing this, but
you are allowed. Just think about being in the cells
and asking to have one of your friends come visit.
Instead of going over anything legal you could just
chat. When I think about it I can't stop smiling.
Imagine some guy trying to impress a girl and he
asks to have her present just to continue courting. If
only I could speak with you I could explain it better.
If only I could write what I think . . .

For my part, I was glad Nathan couldn't write
what he thought. Tall, rangy Nathan, with his
land-roll walk, and the neat gleaming teeth he
was always revealing. Once he'd told me, with that
same smile flashing, 'Of course I try to maintain
this upbeat persona, but I am probably one of the
saddest, *sourest* people you are ever going to meet.'
 'Let's hope so,' I said.

We'd become friends soon after he came to Manchester, while I was still working in the campus bookshop. He appeared at my till late one January afternoon, smiling right at me as he put a pair of snow-frosted gloves down next to his stack of books.

I smiled back, kind of, and then ran the scanner over the following:

Kafka's Diaries Volume 2

The Memoirs of Sherlock Holmes

White Nights

The Green Ray

and

The Crack Up

As he pulled his gloves back on, I cracked.

Nathan was feeling homesick that day, he said. He hugged the carrier bag to his chest as he left.

'I certainly hope these work!' he said, from the top of the stairs.

From the window I watched him stroll down Oxford Road. It was already dark out there. Grey slush hills were heaped in the gutters, and the dirty melt-water ran on the salted tarmac: catching the coloured night-lights and drawing them out. Bus after bus ground slowly past, Magic Buses and Stagecoaches and UK Norths.

★

A new girl had started up on the bookshop's second floor. What was her name? Stacey, maybe. Sarah? It hardly matters. We were never exactly friends. There'd been the usual strained chattiness between us on our first shift together, not much after that; we both would just drift about, take turns standing at the till. Which is what made it odd, when she came and stood next to me at the window then. I didn't like it. I walked off. But as we were about to leave that night, she was at it again, smiling sheepishly and asking me if I had fifteen minutes to go for a cup of tea. She wanted to ask my advice, she said. The idea struck me as so funny, so basically insincere, that I said okay. We put our coats and hats on, and hurried together to a café she knew a few streets away.

'I appreciate this,' she said, as she carried our rattling tray to the back of the room, to a table in the corner.

There, keeping her voice low, she started talking about her fiancé, how he kept getting drunk, getting jealous, smashing things up.

'My Mum hates him,' she said, 'but the thing is, he's on medication, so he's not himself.' Here she smoothed her hair behind her ears, shook her head.

'And then when he stops it's worse. He isn't himself then either.'

I nodded at her, although I had no real experience with what she was talking about.

'And he's so aggressive,' she said, and looked at me expectantly.

I chewed my biscuit and swallowed it.

'In what way? Are you saying he's hit you, or . . . ?'

She nodded.

'Hm. No, not exactly, but there was one time,' and here she leant forward, put her hands flat on the table, 'when he held a steak knife to my throat. For no reason, really.'

She demonstrated for me how he'd clamped his hand over her mouth. All she was then was a pair of wide eyes. A pair of wide eyes trying to back me into saying something concerned. She found it titillating to do that, I suppose. Well, what could I do? I said what I'd been taken there to say. 'Oh no. That sounds wretched. You can't live with someone like that,' I said. 'He might kill you one of these days. They do, you know. They kill you in the end.'

That was the script, after all. She was in the grip of her *amour fou* and I'd been enlisted as an unbeliever. I watched her look furtively around the empty room, smooth her hair again. Of course she looked at me with a quaint kind of pity as she said, 'Oh, I'm not afraid to *die*, Natalie.'

I left that job soon afterwards. For a year or so I just spent my time being poor. There were more forms to fill in, but all in all, I preferred it, reading and writing, falling into debt. It put a funny smile on my face, anyway.

Nathan left Manchester that September. He took me out on his last night, we had a meal in Chinatown, and afterwards went for a walk together along the towpath. All evening he'd been affecting a mood of self-conscious elegy. He'd sighed and frowned. In the restaurant I'd watched him running a finger along the crease lines of the paper tablecloth, as if he were mapping out dead ends. Now, strolling under the stars with his hands thrust deep in the pockets of his chino safari shorts, he said, 'So how's your love life, Natalie?'

'My love life . . . is completely abstract,' I said. It was, too.

'Meaning?' Nathan said.

But I didn't answer his question. I only shook my head. I was drunk, and everything around me and inside me seemed equal in its funny obviousness.

'Say, did I ever tell you that I once dated a girl who didn't kiss?' Nathan said. 'She didn't like it. This was while I was at college in Boulder, dreadfully green, but I thought I was pretty slick. This threw me. At the end of this perfectly choreographed first date, I move in to kiss her, she *recoils*: "I don't kiss," she says. I mean, man, that's my opening paragraph, that's my entrée. You have no idea how I got from that to actually sleeping with this girl.'

'You did sleep with her?' I said.

Nathan laughed his girlish laugh. His teeth glinted.

'I did. Weirdest experience of my life,' he said. Then, 'Hey, I kissed you once.'

I widened my eyes.

'I know you did,' I said.

Nathan walked ahead of me a few steps and then turned to look back at me. He was so tall; he bent down to look at my face.

'Or should I say you kissed me? Natalie, you're blushing. It's embarrassing, I know, but I'm enjoying the embarrassment!'

'Good for you,' I said.

I wasn't enjoying it particularly. Kissing Nathan was an uncomfortable memory for me. I was drunk when I did it, and after I did it, I told him, No, sorry, I don't know why that happened. I pushed him away and laughed, and then pushed him away again. The look on his face wasn't nice. I only laughed out of nervousness. On the walk home that night I carried a sickly, squirming guilt inside me. I remember how I carried it, very carefully, up the stairs to my flat.

And I'd kept his letter, too. Again, I wasn't sure why. Vanity, I suppose. I only read half of it that day on the bedroom floor, and then I scrunched the tissue of paper into a ball, put that back in the envelope and threw it away. I hoped again that he hadn't kept that postcard I'd sent him when I was in a funny mood.

Incidentally – it so happened that I did see that Stacey (or Sarah) again, although circumstances being what they were, we didn't speak. It was a few months after I left work, a dark hour of the early afternoon, and I was on my way to the library. Walking past the town hall, I saw the usual huddle of council workers smoking on the steps of the benefits office, opposite the registry office. They watched without interest, and I turned to look too, as a pale blue Mercedes drew up in front of them, and a young bride ducked out. Stacey hitched up her skirt and hurried across the road. An older woman followed her out of the car. Her mother, I supposed.

★

At the bottom of boxes like this one, there are always chewed pen lids and drawing pins, ancient receipts, yellowing newspaper clippings whose significance isn't obvious. In this case, rattling about amongst all that debris, was a black, label-less audio cassette. I recognised it as the first tape my grandparents tried to make for Bompa Bramwell after he went blind. I'd heard it before, but decided to have another last listen. Sitting up and hunched over all day had given me back-ache; between my shoulders the muscles felt like shrink-wrapped marbles. After I pressed Play, I lay back on the floor, stretched out and working my shoulders around.

There was some hissing and squawking on the tape. Then thirty seconds or so of chopped-up silence. Finally Grandad's voice:

'. . . *and now I'm . . . lying on the floor . . .*' he said.

He had a brisk way of speaking, just a touch of a Scouse accent:

'. . . *with the microphone on the floor about a foot from my mouth. I'm just hoping this is it . . .*'

There was another clunk, then. A change in the texture of the squishy background noise. Grandad again:

'. . . just see if this makes any difference. I'm turning the volume down now . . .'

His voice started to fade away.

'I'm not sure it makes any diff – '

Grandma's shrill voice cut in:

'. . . batteries or mains. We've bought a transformer for it – they're not dear – after we've been caught out with flat batteries once or twice.'

She pronounced it 'flet betteries'. She was brought up in Yorkshire but she spoke like Celia Johnson.

A click, now, and Grandad spoke again:

'After we've been caught out with flat batteries once or twice. Hilda is progressing with her arm exercises, although she's in pain a lot of the time. Each day she progresses with an extra step. Today for instance was the first day she could wash her face with both hands. We go to physiotherapy twice a week. They call it the Pain Clinic. I sit in the car and do the crossword in the Express, while Hilda has her arm stretched.

We bought a swinging settee for the back porch. Hilda calls it a "Swinging Betty". Is that a Yorkshire expression? I've not heard it before.'

There was the tissuey rustle of thin sheets of paper. As I understood it, Grandma wrote the letters and then Grandad read them out.

'I've not heard it before. Anyway, it's making us very hillbilly-ish, as we sit . . . and rock in it . . . and call for more hominy grits!'

An explosion of laughter, there.

'Hilda said I'd look good whittling a stick. Heh!'

Grandad took a moment to calm down.

'I've also made a fountain in the back garden by drilling a hole in the bird-bath and running a nylon pipe underground from the wash-house tap and then up the column of the bird-bath and out through a nozzle. Hilda says I'll soon have to charge people to look round. Luckily Natalie didn't spot the nylon pipe or she'd have had it up. She had to content herself with filling the bird-bath with soil, two stone penguins, two stone frogs, five plastic boats and three plastic ducks. Oh, and she uprooted a plastic heron we have, for good measure.

When she goes home Jane's neighbours will all be retreating inside and locking their front doors until the danger has passed.'

There was the rustle of pages again . . .

'Now, being as I am something of a nutter for stone animals in the garden. Well!'

And he was off.

'He he he! Ha!'

And a wheeze.

'Oh.'

A sigh.

'Excuse me. Just call me the Laughing Policeman.'

And then an endless wheezing, and a chuckle and a splutter. There was a clunk and another clunk.

'Oh, dear. Anyway. Well, when we went to Liverpool a couple of weeks ago Hilda stayed in the car because of her broken arm and also so it didn't get stolen, while I went to order the Swinging Betty. The garden shop had a sale on and on my way out I saw two stone eagles, about a foot high — they were half price, and I thought how good they would look, one each side of our semi-detached stately-home front entrance.

There were only those two left and I didn't want to risk coming back for them so I bought them on the spot. I had only gone a few yards with them, though, when I realised that they wouldn't be the only endangered species if I carried on. So I put one down against a shop window and carried on with the other until the one I had left was just in visibility range. I then put the other eagle down and retraced my steps to pick up the first one. By this time a small knot of people were gazing at me as though it were all some kind of Candid Camera *gimmick. I picked up the first eagle and walked past the other eagle an equivalent distance, depositing it on the pavement before going back to retrieve . . .*

Grandad got the giggles again.

'Excuse me. Settle down now. Ma ha ha ha. Oh, my. I thought I'd be better if Hilda went out of the room . . . . She went out but now I can hear her laughing in the . . .'

There was another clunk. A final clunk. The rest of that tape was quite blank.

After Grandma died, Mum had to clear her house out. She did it quickly, over a weekend, going from room to room. I couldn't help because I didn't know what she wanted to keep, so I just waited in the living room, watched the TV.

By the settee in there Grandma had always kept a margarine tub full of pens to do the puzzles in the paper with. There were dozens of them, mostly the kind you get sent in request letters from charities. Grandma would pick one out and blow on the nib, and then draw zigzags on her pad until the ink came. If the ink didn't come she put the pen back in the tub. She did the cryptic crossword in the *Daily Express*, and always phoned her friend at lunchtime to compare answers.

On the mantelpiece over the gas fire was a

wooden Mexican man, smoking under his red sombrero, holding down the coupons she'd collected; and there was Grandad's old cigarette lighter, a foot-high suit of armour: you had to lift the visor and click the switch at the back. I was always told not to touch it, but that day I sat it next to me on the settee and clicked away, watching the blue spark scribble on the flint.

I helped Mum load the car, and went with her to drop the boxes and bags off at the Macmillan shop in Rock Ferry. Grandma's next-door neighbour helped her lug furniture out to the skip – the bed frame, and the mattress, and the wardrobes. I remember Mum coming inside again afterwards, flush-faced, rubbing her hands on the back pockets of her jeans. I remember her crouching by the freezer with a bin bag next to her. She looked up at me.

'Nearly done now,' she said.

3

Considering my reflection, I closed one eye and then the other. Leaving was a manoeuvre I'd rehearsed so many times, and somehow always just ended up in my flat. Jeane was right. Each escape route led back. The local rail network was like a Möbius strip. How could this be my last day? Queuing by the till, I got transfixed, watching slick little hair switches skip in front of the junior's brush.

A bad excuse for daylight was filling up Deansgate, and there were the usual wet people walking around in it. Clouds billowed indigo against the dulling sky, and in the baskets hanging outside the pub opposite, tiny flowers shuddered, their bitty white petals clasped as if in prayer.

I stayed in the doorway, reluctant to step out. By and by I even saw Jeane across the road. She wore a blank look — fixed and faraway — as she moved over the old, oiled puddles, her arms held out slightly from her sides.

She'd always had that manner about her, that rigorous maladroit poise. Alice in Wonderland, lost, but pressing on. Or maybe more like a clockwork toy, set on its course until someone picks it up and turns it around. She and I had spent a lot of time wandering about this city and writing about it. We wrote about: two precocious holograms; two spooky indigenes running their hands over all the brick walls; two bad aphorists discussing . . . ciphers.

When I first met her she was reading *A Season in Hell*. She carried that book with her as we became friends; a stout little hardback, it looked like a music box. Now as she walked past I stepped back. Did I see her smile to herself, say to herself, *I'm ready for death I'm ready for death*? Or was that in my head?

It was a year since I'd last seen her Mick. My last night out, I think. Refusing to leave the Temple at closing time, he was down on the floor, on his side, spinning and kicking out, spinning and spitting and screaming like a firework.

'This is it!' he kept shrieking. 'This is it!'

And his little legs scrabbled around, and he laughed his chainsaw laugh: 'A-ha-ha-ha-ha-ha!'

★

By the fountain in Albert Square I sat and waited. The wind blew and the pigeons gurgled; they flapped about half-heartedly. Dark spots of rain appeared on the cobbles, and soon cobwebby strands of water were lashing across the cab windscreens. A grey, glittered splatter. I shivered in my thin jacket and looked around. Are there things you're supposed to do when you're about to leave a place? A tour of duty of all the old purlieus? It seemed like vanity to do it and vanity not to.

There was someone I was watching there, anyway: in the Café Italia, someone else I used to know and had ceased to know. He was leaning on his elbows, one hand in his hair, the other holding his small coffee cup up at forehead height. He'd stayed still like that for some minutes, statue-still.

The last time he and I had met up I'd got so drunk I couldn't cross the road. Trying to get home, I just whirled around, doing a monologue at the sky. Of course my face was glowing like a beacon of truth. That was two years ago, a few weeks before Christmas, on one of those brittle autumn evenings that tastes of gunpowder. I remember he kept taking one step out into the traffic and then stepping back, and I made an exasperated face but he wasn't having that. Suddenly there was a hand over my eyes, and one just touching the small of my back, and he was guiding me over. I heard the cars brake and beep, felt the gritted breeze rush by. The hands weren't pressing onto me at all, they were just there, just touching, and then they were gone.

On the steps of my building I stood with my eyes closed and my head tilted up.

'Go to bed, Natalie,' he said.

I didn't move. I opened one eye.

'Oh, for Christ's sake. Are we going to fall out again?' he said.

Apparently we were.

Now I watched him put his cup down, close his folder and push it into his leather satchel. He pushed his chair back a little way and I folded my arms tight as I watched him reach up, put his hands behind his head, and then tilt his head slowly one way, then the other.

He'd done his reading, had his coffee, and so now he was having a stretch. He always did strike me as knowing something I didn't. Once he described a bad few weeks he'd had as being, 'Not a depression exactly . . . but a lull.'

The rain was floating down as he walked off over the slick pavement. A fissure had opened in the clouds, a scarf of amber light in the soft grey. I watched his back, the back of his head; his dark hair fluffed up by the wind.

American Literature made me feel better. Up on the fourth floor of Central Library, I put my shoes under my chair, pulled my legs up and crossed them. I'd spent a lot of time there over the years.

That day, resting my head on my folded arms, it was Joshua Spassky that I thought about. It wasn't a memory, or a speculation; just that as I blinked at the old book spines, I saw him blinking back at me.

I wondered about putting a coin under my tongue, before I went to sleep that night.

4

And then I was at Piccadilly Station, straddling my holdall on a chilly platform thirteen, alternating between yawning and taking sips from a cardboard cup of black tea. Next to me, an efficient-looking woman was making a phone call, tapping her foot on the twitching carpet of rain.

On the other side, a portly man in a suit and a slate-coloured mac leant over to stare poignantly up the tracks. There were parents striding about, too, herding their luggage, herding their children. All this under a sky that was a dimmed white, like clean bone, or old wax, or Tupperware.

My eyes hurt. I shuffled along in the queue to board.

After that there were stockyards, areas of wasteland, old factories. The thin streets around the grouped blocks of flats harboured draughty cafés, laundrettes, darkling pubs; and then the suburbs crowded in, semis with empty drives, empty gardens with mushy lawns and washing lines, patio furniture. I watched all this go by, and the suspense was like an itch, somewhere behind my sternum.

5

The first time I was on a plane Mum held my hand as we taxied down the runway.

'Look out of the window, Natalie,' she said. 'For thirty seconds. You can do it.'

I felt the shudder of take-off and saw the green fields tilt. The wing we were sitting over seemed to flap stiffly, as it carved an arc through smothering clouds. Mum kept her hand on my hand. She looked at me looking out of the frosted-up window.

The book on my knee was a Sherlock Holmes Dad had given me. I'd always spent school breaks with him before, because he wasn't working. He lived near Warrington, in a terrace the colour of dried ketchup, on a street where the kids were always playing out late. Usually we stayed in, though, cooking meals, watching the films he'd circled in the TV guide. One year we went camping in Scotland. We drove through the highlands all day with no radio reception, and

I looked up dutifully every time he spotted an eagle. At night he cooked beans or soup on the small gas ring, and we'd read our books and he'd plan walks with his OS map. He'd died that spring, though, when I was twelve. On Easter Monday he was admitted to hospital with his angina and on the Friday he had a heart attack and died.

For a few hours every evening that week, I'd sat with him while Mum waited downstairs in the WRVS café.

His bed was at the end of the ward. The first night I walked down there, I saw him before he saw me. He was eating his dinner off a tray and wincing at it. His hair was fluffed up at the back.

'Hi, Dad,' I said and I waved for some reason. He looked round, put his fork down, and waved back.

'Sorry about this,' he said, as I sat down. 'Hospitals aren't nice places.'

I was glad when we fell into the same discussion we'd have had on a normal weekend. He'd saved the newspaper, and he went through the international pages with me, pointing out stories of foreign conflicts and saying things like: 'Not within my lifetime, but within yours, this will all reach boiling point. These people will see the consequences of doing this to their young men, putting guns in their hands.'

Or:

'This is just rabidity, you understand. There's no logic. These people have become rabid because of what they've been put through.'

Or:

'Of course you won't find out five per cent of what's really going on in rags like this.'

He'd said all this before.

When I asked how he was feeling, he avoided that question, but his voice gained momentum, again he sounded interested, as he listed the different medicine he was going to have to take from now on. Of one tablet he said, 'It causes mental disturbance, apparently, so that'll be my excuse!'

He said, 'There's no use being squeamish, Natalie,' and he asked me to pass his toilet bag up. I found it in the dresser cupboard, a shabby brown cord case with a snap fastener. He opened it on his lap and pulled things out to show me, to rattle at me.

I wasn't feeling squeamish, exactly. I thought it was interesting. Steradent and Anusol.

'That's what bodies are,' Dad said.

I was still going to school every day. Mum must have told the teachers, because their eyes were expectant. They all kept tilting their heads at me.

I didn't have a particular friend I talked to. Most of the girls in my class had just sat up on their desks and hair-sprayed each other for five years so far as I could tell. Otherwise, there was a constituency of misfits I could have drunk tea with in the canteen: a fat girl, a filthy girl, and a girl from the orchestra with one blind eye and a broad back. They were always nice to each other and to me. Every so often one of them would go over to the Spar for biscuits and magazines. One lunchtime the half-blind girl had told us her boyfriend didn't want her talking to him when he was with his friends. The other two tutted and clucked.

'We need more Digestives for this!' the filthy girl said.

As I'd got older visiting my Dad at the weekends had become more of a chore, and also more of a chess game. I just wanted the time to pass so I could go home, and sit on the settee with Mum and watch the TV, and read a book and have snacks.

One Saturday morning, driving to his house, I'd noticed a pair of tramps fighting on the hump in the middle of a roundabout. I pointed them out, the woman tramp rolling around in the briars while the man tramp kicked her. Dad drove round the roundabout three or four times.

'That's just the way some relationships work, Natalie,' he said. 'There are lots of different kinds.'

He had his left hand on the steering wheel. His other arm was hanging out of the open window. After a moment I said, 'Oh, like you and Mum, you mean.'

Dad didn't take his eyes off the road, though. He only shook his head. He said, 'I don't think that was the reason for the divorce, Natalie. There were deeper, more *psychological* reasons for that. Looking back now, I think it would be more accurate to say that your mother was abusing me.'

I stayed at his house that night, in the spare room with the posters on the wall. In bed, I'd been trying to read but had given up. The book was open on my face and I was blinking over the top of it, too inert to even reach out and switch the light off. Suddenly, though, I saw a large spider hurrying across the ceiling towards me. This wasn't good. I kept my eyes on it as

I eased out of bed; covered my head with both my hands and edged round the wall to the door.

Dad pretended to be irritated that I'd called him.

'Spiders won't hurt you,' he said, huffing up the stairs. 'They're useful to have around. Pest control.'

But when he saw it, squatted on the skirting board now, he said, 'Good God! That is a real mother and father of a size!'

He hit it lots of times with his slipper. I sat up on my bed. I saw its long legs splayed and its body smearing.

'Oh, poor thing!' I said.

Dad lifted his slipper up to me as a joke, and then — just out of spontaneous spite — I froze my face, cringed back against the wall. Well, maybe not that spontaneous. A thought I often had back then was that Dad had to atone for what he'd done to Mum, 'all day, every day, for the rest of his life'.

'Deeper, more psychological reasons,' he'd said. Well, Mum had married him on the rebound, that much was true. At their wedding Grandma made a remark he overheard. Strange that Dad should tell me about that, but he had done, several times, in passing. It was strange, because, really, he used to punch Mum in the face. I'd seen it. Him cracking the back of his hand against her face. I read all the court papers, the solicitors' letters, too, eventually. It all came down to me.

Another incident that comes back: the day he picked me up from school when I wasn't expecting him. He'd looked agitated and I thought, Perhaps he's going to kidnap me. But I got into his car anyway. I had no choice. Dad leant back between the seats and said, 'Natalie, I have to tell you that your Nana O'Flaherty died last night.'

His voice cracked when he said that, and he gripped the headrest he was leaning on.

Just a few years later it was him who was ill, and looking thinner all the time. His eyes were getting bigger. Every night I tried to avoid them, sitting on the edge of the chair by his hospital bed, holding the sides of my seat. I told him about school, hamming up how bad my teachers were because I knew he liked to shake his head over that. I lied and said one of them saw me reading *The Brothers Karamazov*. I said they seemed really surprised, in fact, 'really put out'. Dad raised his eyebrows and nodded, hurrying to swallow the food he was chewing. He reached out for his tumbler of water.

That was on the last night. He talked a lot then. He told me about the Christian Brothers who ran his school. A vicious creed, by all accounts, wielding canes and switches. He told me a punishment they often used was to have a boy stand still and silent in a small chalk circle at the front of the room.

'Christians!' he said.

His mouth was so dry. His, pale, scabby lips brushed together as he spoke; his tongue ticked in his mouth as he told me, 'On the school bus the older boys were always quoting Stanley Unwin skits. I never thought he was funny myself. I just couldn't see it.'

Later still, he lowered his voice to complain about how the doctor smirked at his questions.

'It's a disgrace,' he said.

There was his bright baggy face and his soft white hair. His eyes watered constantly. This discharge seemed sticky, like thin phlegm, like a glaze when he wiped his face with the huge handkerchief he kept.

'Sorry, Natalie,' he said, 'Could you pass me that water. Thank you, Natalie.'

Mum woke me to tell me he was dead. She'd

brought me breakfast on a tray at 4 a.m.

'Are you okay?' she said.

I nodded. I was fine. I couldn't eat too much though. That day and for weeks afterwards my stomach felt as if it was filled with wet gravel. All through the holiday Mum took me on I felt ill. I felt a concentrated illness.

Steradent and Anusol. That's what bodies are. Did he imagine he was going to die that week, though? Was he trying to make me feel better? It was intrusive to speculate. Self-serving, too. But I did speculate.

Anyway, they're all dead now. Mum's dead. She took nine months to die. Again, there was only me with her. That's how life had set her up. And I didn't know how to behave. I felt too hysterical, too disgusted. I felt as though there was a nuclear light in my head that I couldn't shut off.

For a few weeks, while she was still working, I started cooking her dinner. When she got home I'd make her sit on the settee and then I'd wheel in Grandma's hostess trolley. There was a creepy piece of equipment.

I was picturing myself like that again: standing in the doorway, watching her eat — when right on cue, my meal on a tray appeared. A woman with a chignon and drawn-on eyebrows handed it across to me.

'You're the vegetarian,' she said.

6

More lugging of my bag next. It was getting heavier; even after a short walk, a cold pain gripped at my back. I did feel frightened, half-stunned; I tried not to look either, and just keep on going through the correct channels towards the exit.

Out on the concourse, I put my bag between my feet, and tried to decide what to do. The wind was snagging my hair into my eyes and people were huffing as they had to walk around me. Was it worth taking a cab? Or one of these silver coaches? I didn't know how much time I had.

I did take a taxi, in the end. It was a fast, bumpy ride across the bridge; then a crawl through wide, jammed streets.

Penn Station was underground, clammy, filled with the sound of suitcase wheels on uneven tiles, the soft shuffle of the flickering departure board. I sat down there and waited.

I left the city that afternoon, passed through another, and another. Only as evening fell was the train finally clacking through the rust belt. There uneven fields stretched to meet a mauve sky; huge silos stood next to farmhouses; church steeples poked out from clapboard towns. As the sun went down its fierce light glimmered and guttered on sprawling, muddy creeks; and we tumbled on, into the black night.

After one stop an old man asked if he could join me. He stood swaying in the aisle with half a sub sandwich in one hand and a box of cards in the other.

'Go for it,' I said.

He breathed laboriously, as he clipped his table down, shuffled the greasy pack. His thin hair was combed back in wavering tracks. The skin on his face was like the leather on a worn-out boxing glove. We played gin rummy.

'It's a waiting game,' he told me.

Outside was only an endless forest; the occasional water tower visible amongst the trees' shaggy silhouettes, like a rusty Tin Man head, or a hovering UFO, a bread bin on stilts.

The hours wore on. Strolling up and down, I sipped from a beaker of black tea. There was cool air between the carriages, a fusty, burnt warmth inside them. I found a strange newspaper scattered on one table, gathered it up and took it back to my seat; read it cover to cover by the high, yellow reading light. For an hour or so, leaning against the scratchy curtain, I closed my eyes, concentrated on various dreams.

That Eden had a terminus however, and I had to throw myself down there. I landed awkwardly next to my holdall.

And night turned to day, and finally a tiny plane bore me up; buzzing like a midge it hoisted its way into the sky. I watched its †-shaped shadow skim the clouds, fall down skittering on the fields and the foothills.

When I woke – half woke – it was to find myself sprawled improbably on one of two double beds in a hotel room, with one arm dead, and my every other muscle aching as if a vital chemical had been siphoned from it. I could barely sit up to take my shoes off. I was like a wound trying to peel itself off a sticking plaster. The one dim thought in my head: what might I eat for breakfast? Hallucinating grapefruit juice, I again fell asleep.

7

The torn paper silhouettes of the Blue Ridge Mountains receded into a pale sky. For a while I stood squinting at this view.

The walkway I was on ran the length of the back of the hotel. It overlooked a cramped patio, where there was a small kidney-shaped pool, in shadow now, only three-quarters filled up. A breeze was picking at its surface; these shivers passed through the dull turquoise water. A couple of plastic sun-loungers were stacked up in one corner down there, too; a snake-coil of thick hose sat by a rusted tap.

Like the rest of the building the wall around the patio was painted gravy brown, with maroon trim. Behind it I could see the bus-station concourse, a car-repair shop, an empty cross-roads, all this loosely rigged with telephone wires, electrical wires, a set of dangling traffic lights.

★

A bookshop seemed like a good place to wait. I found one close by, on Lexington, two large rooms full of shady corners and spider plants; there was already a handful of browsers in there, strolling and squatting.

On a low chair in Literary Biography, I spent some time looking through the weightless old hardbacks; just skim reading, various glum melo-dramas, cavalier escapades . . . I took down *The Other Side of Paradise* and turned the woody pages over in chunks, looking for the photo-graphs. There he was: '*Grove Park Inn, Asheville, 1937.*' In a tweed jacket and a short striped tie: F. Scott Fitzgerald. He was half-smiling, he was mid-fidget. The flash had flashed and caught him that way.

Underneath was a picture of the fire at the Highland Hospital: white flames inside the building's grey skeleton. '*Zelda's locked room was on the third floor,*' the caption said.

I turned back a few pages, and again, there was Scott, a young man now, with glossy, centre-parted hair, his eyes gleaming blandly. I put my finger on his forehead, and I thought about — how people have to end up.

'*That's what bodies are, Natalie.*'

'*Love isn't a matter of logistics.*'

But did they mean the same thing or the opposite thing?

The lanky young man at the cash desk leant on his elbows and scratched at his sea-spongy blond beard.

Outside, I continued to wander up and down the broad, sloping streets; across the tawny tarmac in the hot, soft breeze. The sky seemed limitless. It really did. But it was 10.15, and Joshua would be here soon. Or at least, he would be or he wouldn't be.

8

There were half a dozen people waiting at the bus station, smoking, pacing aimlessly around. Others looked like more long-term residents. They stretched out slumbering on the benches, with perishing plastic bags scrunched up at their feet. One gaunt old man had a radio on his chest. He was turning the dial very slowly: voices and music came and went. I sat down against a wall, but soon felt restless and stood up again. I started pacing around too.

Until I saw the bus approaching, sunlight glinting on its silver flanks. It swung around the last corner, slowing down, and pulled into bay number four.

Through the filmy reflections on the tinted windows, I saw the bustle of people's middles, as they reached up or down for their bags. And then the engine shut down, and then the door popped open sluggishly.

Exposed one by one to the pale day, each new

face squinted; steps faltered. There was a raggedy young family, collecting suitcase after suitcase from the hold, dragging them clear. And later a rather wide old lady, with a tissue bunched in her hand. She blocked the door for a while, blotting her slick forehead, looking around for someone she knew. I saw Joshua waiting behind her.

He needed a coffee, that was the first thing he said, after our hug.

9

Now I watched him yawn again, click his jaw.

He looked dazedly up at the girl who came over with the coffee jug, and dazedly down at his cup as she filled it. I moved my cup forward, too.

Taking a first cautious sip of his drink, Joshua squinted back at me.

'Oh, God,' he said.

With one hand pushed into his sweaty hair, one flat on the tabletop, he did look as though he might slide forward and sleep. The way he was moving there, flexing his neck, he looked like the last chunk of ice-lolly, about to fall off the stick.

'So, it's taken me weeks to get here, you know?' he said. 'It's taken me weeks, and it's cost me – thousands of dollars.'

He looked at his left hand on the table – he was spreading his fingers – and then back at me.

'Really,' I said. 'What's that, in therapy?'

'Therapy? No, just bus fares, you know, and candy, sodas, a couple dozen sandwiches, potato chips. I bought a newspaper . . .'

He interrupted himself with another yawn; covering his mouth with his hand, he widened his eyes in a merry way. I shook my head.

His same old hat was on the table next to him, and I picked it up and looked at it.

When he and I had first met, five years ago, I was twenty-two years old, and I'd just finished my first novel. He was in Manchester overseeing a production of his third play. In the Contact Theatre bar he was introduced to me as 'the man himself'. He'd winced at that, as he leant across to shake my hand. And then he'd continued to look at me, from his corner seat, in a weary, beleaguered, insolent way. I was looking at him in an unusual way, too. The posters behind him were all announcing:

Joshua Spassky's
'EXPECTORATION'

Now I took a sip of my coffee. It spilled over my fingers, into the saucer, as I put the cup down again.

'Are you okay?' Joshua said.

I sucked my sore tongue-tip and nodded.

I said, 'I'm fine. So – what are you writing these days, Joshua?'

He took a moment before answering.

'What am I writing?' he said. 'Oh. I have a couple things half done. This one I'm finishing up now is called *The Box of Bad Endings*. That's for a theatre in Chicago. I'm going down there for casting next month. It's only a one-act. It's not a million miles from what I've done before. Starting out I thought it might be, but it's not.'

'And – is it profoundly sorrowful?'

'I don't know if sorrowful's the word. There's a certain sense of pointlessness,' he said, and he scratched under his chin. He went on, 'I guess the way I've been putting it is like this: that there are a lot of lines in the play, but you could para-phrase most of them as "I'm fucked", "I'm fucked too", "We're fucked", "We fucked it up and there's no way back". That's what can happen to people, after all. So it's just about that. And about this . . . basic incompatibility between men and women.'

'I see,' I said.

He looked at me, steadily, lazily.

I sipped some more of my coffee, took a moment to swallow it. I said, 'I used to know a couple who were like a one-act play.'

'You did?'

'A long time ago. I used to go round to theirs for tea, and then I'd spend the whole hour dodging meaningful glances, having drinks pressed on me to make them feel better, and generally waiting for one of the company to go out into the hall and shoot themselves.'

'Ya, that sounds about right,' Joshua said.

He uncurled the fingers of the hand he was leaning on and laid them against his cheek.

On the table between us were a condiment set, a steel napkin dispenser and a glass sugar shaker. With his free hand, Joshua touched each of these items in turn.

'How about you?' he said. 'You're writing another book? Oh. Excuse me a second.'

He'd asked the waitress for a refill, and now he smiled up at her. I looked, too: she was a solemn young hippy, tanned and tattooed, dressed in fading remnants, a grey wool ski hat. Only a few wisps of her dark hair were visible, at the nape of her neck; some stuck to her lips. She filled both of our cups, right up to the brim.

'Well, it's finished now,' I said. 'My book. It's

called *A Shag on the Horizon*. It's a book about hope. Everyone who reads it is going to vomit with grief. Hopefully.'

'And is that set in Manchester, again?' he said, looking back at me now.

'No. Not really. It's not that kind of book. It's set – in my head.'

'Oh. Well. I'll look forward to reading that.'

'I wouldn't go that far. Manchester. I had to get away from there. Everything had reached an odd pitch. In concert. It was deranging me, but slowly. My book opens like that. The first line is, "Every building drips with the thrush of failed love."'

'With the . . . ?'

'With the thrush. The thrush of failed love.'

'I see,' he said. 'Well, I guess it's good to have a holiday from that.'

I nodded.

'Yes, it is.'

He tugged at the hair over his ear as he looked at me. He had dull, red-brown hair, parted low on the left, growing out, curling up. He had broad, Slavic cheekbones, flushed cheeks, a ruddy, red nose.

He smiled to himself, and tilted his head, and then rubbed his eyes.

'So, I guess one idea I had was for us not to get too drunk over the next few days?' he said.

'Okay.'

'I mean, we always get *so* drunk. I'm not saying we shouldn't have a drink, but if we get really drunk, we're going to lose the opportunity to talk to one another. I mean, that's happened before. And if we don't talk, you know, what's the point?'

He rested his chin on his fist now, and squinted at me.

'I'm not sure,' I said. 'As for drinking, I've given up at the moment. So.'

'Really, you did?'

I nodded.

'Oh. Well, that's good, I guess,' he said. 'I've thought about that.'

'It's not bad. It's been a year or so. If you want to have a drink, though, that's okay. Obviously, we've never not been drunk around one another.'

'That's true,' he said. 'That's why I was having this whole drunk/sober debate with myself these past couple days, and I kind of thought sober. Sober-ish. I mean, I'm a little drunk now, but there wasn't much else to do on that coach. A year. Gosh. What prompted your um . . . turnaround?'

'Oh. Lots of things. I could go into it. Is that what you mean by talking?'

'I don't know. Could be.'

'Could be,' I said. 'Have you noticed how our conversations have always tended to this point, though? They become these peculiar confessionals.'

'Do they?'

'I've noticed that they do. Confessional might be the wrong word. Anyway, as to why I stopped drinking, I kept waking up in a wet bed – was one reason.'

Joshua didn't say anything. He looked very tired. Every now and then he did this, I remembered, he showed his age. The lines that ran under his eyes sloped down as they trailed off.

I leant back and looked around the room. The girl who'd served us was cleaning the huge brass coffee machine, scrubbing around a ragged sticker that said, **Friends Don't Let Friends Drink Starbucks**.

'Do you want to go back to this hotel, then?' I said, turning back to Joshua. 'You'll like it. I'd call it a cast-concrete hive.'

He nodded. 'Yeah, I am pretty exhausted. I feel grubby, too.'

As he slid out of his seat and pulled his rucksack out from under the table, he said, 'And I meant to ask you, incidentally, why are we here?'

'This was your idea, though. I just showed up.'

He pulled his rucksack up onto his shoulder, picked up his hat and followed me out.

'No, I meant, why here? Why would you want to meet here?'

'Oh. Well, it was arbitrary, more or less,' I said, turning back to face him. He was only the same height as me.

'I just liked the sound of it,' I said. 'April in Asheville. Don't you think?'

10

Buckets of dried cement mix flanked the entrance to the Days Inn; parts of the small lobby were hidden behind paint-splattered sheets, and from the holes left by missing ceiling tiles, balls of coloured wire hung stiffly, nest-like. Carpentry noises came from unseen places. On the corkboard by the lift, gold plastic letters spelled out: PLEASE EXCUSE OUR APPEARANCE. None of these letters was stuck on quite straight. Another injunction, pinned beneath that one, inscribed with some force on a cardboard shirt back:

IMPORTANT NOTICE
Residents are <u>not permitted</u> to take locals up to their rooms as guests.

The snowy-haired man at reception smiled vaguely at the fax he was reading. It was a smile that said: *If that's really what you want . . .* As the phone started to ring, he reached out and put a consoling hand on it.

The first thing Joshua did, when we got into our room, was to lie face down on one of the beds, groaning and sighing. I sat down next to him. There was his narrow back, his worn-out black leather belt, the sliver of pale, freckled skin exposed where his plaid shirt was pulled up. He rolled over onto his side, groaned again, and pushed his hair up out of his face with his right hand.

'Oh, Natalie,' he said. 'You know, I think spending two days on a bus is one of the worst ideas I've had. A classic example of something that wasn't as romantic as I thought it might be? I was bored after a half-hour.'

He sat up then, and leant forward to unlace his shoes, push them off. He lifted his bag up onto his knees, and started looking through it, frowning as he reached deep inside. Finally he pulled out a bottle and handed it to me. A half-full bottle of Jack Daniel's, engine-warmed, sticky. I unscrewed it, waited a few seconds and then passed it back to him. We were sitting on the edge of the bed I hadn't slept in, facing the half-drawn curtains and the quietly chugging air-conditioning unit. Some time after his swigful, Joshua said, 'So, we haven't talked about this yet, but I guess I should say I'm sorry. You know, for not showing up last year?'

'Oh, okay,' I said.

Again he handed me the bottle, and then continued, 'I mean, I felt bad. For not calling. It was – inconsiderate.'

He had his head tilted to one side, hair falling over his eyes. His voice was a laden baritone.

'Well. It's a bit late to go over all that now,' I said.

His expression didn't change.

I lifted up the bottle, touched my finger on its lip and tasted it. I've never liked whiskey. That's what I thought then, and a moment later, too, holding what I'd swigged in my mouth, feeling it scorch my gums. No, I don't like this, I thought, and so I just leant forward, letting the drink flow out and back into the bottle. It was then that I felt the soft prickle of Joshua's two-day stubble as he kissed me under my right eye. Various thoughts went through my mind when he did that. Various competing impulses. He had his hand on the back of my neck.

'You are so stunning,' he was saying. 'So important to me.'

He leant over to kiss me again. He looked

pious, childish like that, with his eyes closed. What could I do, though? We kissed for a while. His mouth had the same old sour tang, the taste of old coins. I took my dress off and he took his shirt off. He leant over me in the gloomy light and I felt very tranquil then.

And clamped against him as he fell asleep; my face pressed into the tickly, clammy pit of his chest. My thoughts didn't extend beyond that. I breathed in and breathed out.

Waking up, Joshua clicked his tongue, made growly noises. He exhaled heavily into my neck and groped blindly at my backside. Finally he shuffled off to the bathroom, hunched up and confused, wearing a cape made of a blanket. I heard him take a stop-start piss, flush the toilet. Listening to him shower, I stretched under the covers. I could see my reflection in the large mirror, and in the blue-grey TV screen.

With his hair wet and combed back, Joshua's face seemed strangely exposed. There was steam coming off his skin, too, floating up from his freckled shoulders. He blinked at me, and looked slightly nervous, I thought, as he knelt down to look in his bag for a pair of pants.

'I'm kind of embarrassed by these,' he said,

frowning down at the checked boxer shorts he was pulling on. 'They're too big. I guess I bought the wrong size.'

He came and stood by the bed so I could see. He had his hands by his sides; his stomach stuck out like a toddler's. In profile it was like a stretched bow.

'Yes. It looks like you're wearing a kilt,' I said.

Joshua shook his head, then he pushed me onto my back, and lay on top of me for a while, on top of the sheet, between my legs, and holding himself up on his elbows. He huffed at the head-board and looked abstracted. Water was trickling off the spikes of hair that had fallen onto his forehead.

I moved my hands to his lower back. It was slim, and smooth save for the straggly patch of hair in the dip where those shorts were pulled up to. We lay there, inert. I looked up at him, staring closely at his face: the scored lines at his temples, the thicker red skin around his nose. He kept closing his eyes then opening them. Finally he stopped supporting himself, and let his whole warm dead weight press on me. Now his head was next to my head, but facing down. He let out a weary sigh.

After he rolled off, he lay next to me, squinting

at me. He pulled the sheet down and looked at my boobs. He poked at them, squeezed one as though it was a car-horn, and then pulled the sheet back up and tucked it carefully into place.

'So are you sure you haven't fallen in love with anyone else since we last met?' he said.

I shook my head.

'I'm sorry I didn't ask you to come in the shower with me.'

'I'm never going to get in a shower with you, Joshua.'

'You're not? Why's that?'

'I'm a serious person. Look at this face. I don't do lather. Me in the shower with you would be – a festival of self-consciousness.'

'You're a serious person?' he said. 'Oh. I'm not. You know.'

He moved some hair out of my eyes, held a switch of it between his fingers and examined it.

11

The evening sun cast a golden pall over down-town, as we walked out together, holding hands. In the park we passed through, there were a few hippies sitting around, legs crossed, leaning back on their hands. One was tapping out a fast beat on a little wooden drum. This funny sound jiggled around us.

Some of the trees were still in bud, and there the impression was of a green mist hanging around the new twigs. Others, already in blossom, had rained petals, and these lay like rag rugs on the soft, trim lawns. The gentle breeze was charged with the scent of spring flowers.

'Do we have a plan?' Joshua said.

'Yes, we're going to join those fellows on the grass,' I said. 'Did you not bring your bongos?'

'I didn't. I thought I could just use yours.'

'Oh no,' I said. 'It's started.'

Joshua's hat was pushed back on his head and

damp licks of his schoolboy hair were curling out in front of his ears.

We walked on.

I said, 'What do you think of this place, anyway? Have you been around here before?'

'No. I never travelled in the South. I think it's the one place I haven't been. Seems like a nice town. Laid back.'

'Well, it's kind of Haight-Ashbury, isn't it? Hippies. What are they up to? Anyway, it's a nice location. I haven't been in the countryside for years. Not that this is countryside, but – out there.'

'Yeah, I'm not such a fan of the 'great outdoors', or whatever. I grew up with it, so.'

'It's nice on a cinema screen,' I said. 'I like Tarkovsky. I like *Tess*. And from a train window, too. The view from the train down to London is okay. I like farm animals: sheep that stand stock-still and staring. And cows, when they're lying down, that's funny. I remember my Mum taking me to a city zoo once, which was basically a goat to pet and a rabbit to hold. She lifted me up so I could reach over and pat this old goat's bony nose. Maybe if I could drive I'd like to drive through the countryside.'

'Ya, that's pretty weird that you can't drive,' Joshua said.

'Is it? Well, it's too late for me to learn now, I think. I daydream, anyway. I'd end up running over some kids and a gran.'

'Okay. I'd hate for you to do that.'

Joshua stopped here, and bent down to tie his shoelace. I kissed the back of his neck. Standing up again, he said, 'If this makes you feel any better, though, I guess they won't be letting me near a car for a while, either. I have my second DUI – that's driving under the influence – hearing next month.'

'Yes, you said you were going to court. What happened there?'

'Oh, it was so stupid,' he said, 'because although I'd had some drinks, I was far from drunk. Basically, I was weaving all over the road, but just for fun. It was 4 a.m., the street was empty, so I was playing around. But this girl I was with, she was all, 'Oh Jay, stop it! You're drunk! Stop the car!' And then what do you know, the cops pull up, out of nowhere. I figure someone in one of these houses was watching.'

'And they arrested you?'

'Ya, they had me doing all kinds of tests: walk

down this line, stand on one leg, say the alphabet backwards starting at Q. It was ridiculous.'

We were in the town square – Pack Square – in front of a low-rise, bronze-glass tower and a fountain; plumes of white water falling down into a shallow pool. It was a nice spot to sit, on a curlicued iron bench, opposite an art museum, across from a row of glowing little restaurants, and with the breeze coming down from the mountains, sprinkling mist on the backs of our arms.

I felt very companionable with Joshua, then. He had his arm around me, his fingers on my shoulder. I stroked his other hand, lifted it up and bent those fingers back and forth. Around his tanned wrist were tied a thin black ribbon and a sink-plug chain. They'd been there for as long as I'd known him. New additions this time were the plastic rings from the top of a four-pack of beer. I twisted them around his wrist.

The high, cloudless sky was changing; dusky turquoise becoming vivid mauve, while the ridge of mountains became black. All around the square, tall street-lights fizzed on haltingly. I breathed in the fresh air, and leant back against the bench boards, and felt okay.

Joshua reached up and scratched the back of his head.

'So here's something I've been meaning to ask you, Natalie,' he said. 'You know the night we met?'

I nodded once.

'When we first made love?'

'Yes.'

He huffed. He said, 'Did you feel something then, like, I don't know, transcendence?'

He turned and frowned at me. He had his head tilted.

'Transcendence,' I said. 'Yes, of course. That was the whole problem.'

'But I wonder if it was maybe because of the time when we met?'

'Okay. Go on.'

'I just mean that we were both quite, I don't know, *low*, at that point. I was really depressed. I was as depressed as I've ever been, actually.'

'It's possible,' I said.

He shrugged.

'These are just some things I've considered,' he said, taking his hat off now, shoving a hand back through his hair. 'When I've thought about that night.'

On the bench next to us, a young man in a soldier's beige fatigues had been smoking a cigarette. He dropped it now, and hastily ground it out under his boot toe, as a stern middle-aged man walked purposefully towards him. The soldier moved his kitbag off the bench and propped it up on the floor, and the older man nodded grimly at him before sitting down.

They sat like that for a while, both looking straight ahead.

The older man was wearing shorts and sandals, a starched white T-shirt. His legs and arms were a baked reddish-brown. Glasses hung on a cord around his neck.

The soldier looked to be about seventeen years old. He had a chubby face, sleepy, slow-blinking eyes. Ripe little pips of acne glowed dully on his temples and chin. Finally, leaning forward, the older man coughed drily, and then said, 'That uniform for real?'

'Oh. Yes, sir, it is.'

'You're not playing dress-up?'

'No, sir,' he looked down at himself, 'This is for real.'

'You home on leave?' the man said.

'Yes, sir, I just – I got in a half-hour ago. I'm waiting for my Mom to finish her shift over there.'

'I see. How long you home for?'

'Um. Just a few days. I –'

'Just a few days.'

'Well, my father passed away, so I –'

'Compassionate leave. I'm sorry to hear that.'

The soldier nodded. He squinted and shrugged.

'Well, when I was about your age, my Dad died. And then my Mom died about a month later.'

'Oh, man.'

'Yip.'

In the pause that followed, the soldier looked over at the café where he'd said his mother worked.

'So you're looking after the family now,' the older man said.

'Oh. I don't know about that . . . my parents were living apart anyways, so . . .'

'Your Mom's holding up?'

'My Mom? I think she's, you know. She just needed some help with organising the funeral, and his house where he lived . . .'

The older man nodded.

'Well, funerals are easy to plan,' he said. 'You just have to keep a tight hold of your wallet, is the thing.'

'Yes, sir, I think she's been trying to do that.'

'You have to make sure she does. I experienced this myself, because I lost my daughter a few years back.'

70

'Oh, man.'

'She took her life, so –'

'Oh, boy.'

'Yeah. It's rough stuff. Rough stuff.'

The old man eased his hand into his shorts' back pocket now, frowning up at the sky as he did so. He tugged out a battered wallet and rifled slowly through it. Finally he handed the soldier a card.

'Well, that's my name and address right there,' he said. 'You recognise that address? It's not too far away. I want you to feel free to knock on my door if you need anything.'

'Thank you, I appreciate that,' the soldier said, squinting at the card.

'Well, I'm proud to meet you,' the older man said. 'I certainly am. I'm only sorry it's in these circumstances.'

The soldier smiled quite awkwardly.

'Yeah. I like coming home, but not like this.'

'If you need anything, though, you have my number now. Or you can knock on my door. I figure if you can help George I can help you. George, who I'm a big fan of, incidentally.'

'Oh, yes, sir, me too.'

'He's great, isn't he?'

'I have some photos.' The boy leant down to

his bag, before sitting up again. 'I sent them home, though. From Thanksgiving? You know he came out on Thanksgiving.'

'Yeah. What a thing to do. You were there? That's great. I mean, what's that other fellow, that other guy, you see him doing that?'

'No, sir. I don't think so.'

'I don't think so. Now tell me something else. You like bikes?'

'Bikes? Yes, sir. I have two bikes.'

'You do? Well, I have three bikes. The truth is I moved to Asheville to ride my bikes. It's heaven. The roads around here are great. I have friends calling up saying, "We want to come to Asheville, what are the best roads?" I say, "Man, every road is great!" You know Highway 63?'

'Yes, sir.'

'That's a great road. But all the roads are great. That's what I like about Asheville. Great people. Live and let live. Great roads. Say, do you need a ride anywhere now?'

'No thank you. My Mom will be done soon. But I appreciate that.'

'Okay. Well, you just let me know. You've got my card there. I'm pleased to have known you.'

'Thank you, sir.'

With that, the man stood up. He crossed the

twilit square, got into his large car, and rolled away. The soldier looked blankly ahead. After a moment he yawned – with his mouth and eyes closed, I saw his nostrils flare – and then he set about finding another cigarette.

12

Under the mild yellow glow of the bedside lamps
I was lying with Joshua Spassky.

We faced each other on a stack of thin
pillows.

'I've been thinking recently,' he said, 'that I
should stop dating girls who aren't intelligent.'

'Sounds like a plan.'

'I'm just flat out bored with history repeating
itself.'

'Tell me about it.'

He reached up and scratched his cheek, gave
a good scratch to where his beard was coming
through again.

'In the last five years,' he said, 'I guess I've
dated five different women, and each time, I
look back and think, What did I get out of
that?'

He rubbed his hand over his face.

'Being alone is just so tough, though. That's
the problem. I know you have this thing of never

74

really dating people, but I don't know how you do it. I wish I could be like that.'

'Well – I'm sure you don't.'

'I don't like to sleep alone, is my basic fix. I can take or leave sex. I don't care about that so much. But I don't like being in bed on my own. Sometimes I more or less refuse to do it, actually. I'll hold myself upright on the mantelpiece, and drink and just not go to bed. I'll watch any kind of TV, drink until I'm asleep . . .'

He shrugged. What he was saying was familiar, but compelling, and he looked very attractive, tucked up there, musing to himself.

'Like I was at my parents' place in Miami last month,' he said, 'and after this girl I was with left, I thought I'd stay on and do some work, and I was writing in the daytime okay, but at night, I couldn't handle it. I was phoning everyone.'

'That's when you phoned me.'

'Well, I'd been meaning to call you for a while.'

'Okay.'

'But the reason I'm telling you this is because – the reason Connie left, was that I was saying all this exact same stuff to her – just about, What am I getting out of this? I thought we should split but she was pretty adamant that we stay together. I don't know. She went home. So we're on a time-out, now. I guess I should tell you that. I figured she was right. It wasn't logical for me to permanently split with her. That would be, you know, it would make me feel better for a while, but then, I couldn't handle being alone long term. She said that to me and she was right.'

'I see,' I said.

But again, what he was saying hardly seemed relevant. It was a native noise, wasn't it? Like a cat's purr or a twitting bird. Sometimes he just made his noises and I made mine. It wasn't true, for instance, that I didn't date people. Every now and then I had. The last one, I finished with last year, when Joshua said he wanted to come and stay. That was a decision I took, and not much of a decision, all told.

Now he pulled me closer. He slipped one fuzzy leg up between my legs. For a good while we lay like that, looking at each other quite steadily. Each time I smiled, he smiled back. Childishly. Like a mirror. And when I frowned.

Finally I had to ask him, 'When we're looking at each other like this, do you ever . . . are you talking to me in your mind at all? Quite often when I'm looking at you I'm talking to you in my mind.'

He frowned, took a moment to reply.

'I guess,' he said, 'or maybe I'm more just thinking, talking to myself. Just then I was thinking, you know, Gosh, she's really quite young, isn't she?'

'Really?'

'Yeah. I don't know. You look young. Sometimes you look older. What are you now, twenty-seven?'

'That's right,' I said. 'The years are going by. I'm afraid of ageing, too. It terrifies me.'

'Really? I don't think I care too much about that. Maybe I used to.'

'Well, I care. I don't think I'll find any consolations, is the thing. There'll just be pain and loss. I won't look like myself. Sometimes when I think about it, it's like it's already happened. Some nights I can't sleep because I'm worried about being put in a home; with my face sagging off, my flesh being like spaghetti dough. Another fear I have is that when I go for a smear test the nurse will look up me and scream; she'll just start screaming. I'm in a constant, low-level, vivid panic about these things.'

'See, now I'm getting scared, too,' Joshua said.

'I'm sorry,' I said. I looked down between us. 'We are both in these semi-serviceable young bodies now, I suppose.'

Joshua shook his head.

I reached over him to click the lights off, and we adjusted ourselves to get more comfortable. His hairy stomach rustled against me. His skin was hot and dry.

He coughed.

I sniffed.

After a while he said, 'Hey. Are you still awake?'

13

There I was. Leaning over a steep precipice.

It had been my idea, to come this way. After lunch we'd walked out to the ABC store to get some more drink – they didn't sell spirits in town – and then we just kept going. The wide road had dipped, and rose steeply, and dipped again, as we went on into the dark green, shouldering hills. We'd passed two steak-houses and a tyre shop; crossed an abandoned car yard, where wrecks with popped hoods sat gawping in tall, tickling grass. We'd passed a sprawling hospital complex, and then an adjunct facility, whose brass plate announced: FERTILITY CLINIC.

And the further we'd walked, the more our pavement had dwindled, to a cursory ledge, to nothing, and so we stepped over the barrier and picked our way along the embankment instead, the slope of scrub beneath the dense fir woods. Joshua went first. Small trucks rumbled past us, their rear ends sashaying. SUVs slid more decorously around the corners, leaving the blare of their horns dying out in their wake. This was the Swannanoa Road, where we stopped to look down at the river. We leant over the wooden railing. The water looked so far away it seemed static, caught; the milky froth netted over flat boulders like a cataract. The rushing sound came up to us, though, the distant din. This noise, and the fresh smell of wet stone, and a hint of spray. I looked hard, and made out the hanks of bright grass the water tugged at, and the stray branches that spun like clock hands in the shallows.

We walked on. The afternoon sun was pale and intense. My lungs felt packed with this stiff light. It hurt my sinuses.

Joshua, up ahead of me, sometimes took off his hat and fanned himself with it, sometimes held his arms out as though he was on a high wire. He had a strange walk, a rigid kind of amble, always with his head tilted up and to one side.

The Carmike 10 Cinema was a neo-classical hutch, in black glass and breezeblocks. It shimmered on the far side of a large, empty car park. Joshua turned and waited for me there. He kicked at the kerb, and when I caught up, he got me in a headlock, ground his fist into the top of my head. He did smell nice, herbal and sporty.

As we walked arm in arm, I said, 'The first time my Dad took my Mum out, they went to see *Marathon Man*.'

'Oh yeah?' Joshua said, offering me his bottle. I shook my head. 'That's a great film,' he said.

'It is, except my Mum was squeamish – she used to cross the road if we were near a butcher's. So on this date, she had to leave in the scene with the dentist's drill, because she thought she'd faint. She went and sat on the floor in the foyer with her head between her knees. I always used to picture her like that. Sitting on the carpet and wheezing. And picture Dad too, of course, still inside, still looking up at the screen. Poor fucker.'

Joshua nodded as he studied the show times.

'Natalie,' he said, 'every film that's on is really bad.'

'Oh,' I said. I looked where he'd been looking. 'You're right.'

We passed into the shadowy foyer; shivered as our sweat dried.

★

With my hands full, my wallet on top of the popcorn, I watched Joshua queue for tickets. He stood with his hands by his sides, looking up at the board. His red hair was sweaty and curly. His stuck-out stomach pulled his T-shirt into pinwheels. His T-shirt had a picture on it of Leonard Cohen eating a banana.

'Look at all this,' I said, walking over quickly. 'I feel like Caligula.'

Once we'd sat down, I poured most of his new bottle into the Coke bucket I'd half emptied down the Ladies' room sink.

Joshua sighed.

'Oh, I love to drink, Natalie,' he said. 'I respect your abstinence, but I'm going to do it as much as possible, all day, every day, until it kills me.'

Each time he bent down to the straw I kissed his neck. I kept my hand on his arm all through the film. I kept seeing things on the screen that were like him, too: a grandad on a porch, a boy with a grazed knee, a little leaping dog. Everything can't be him, Natalie, I thought. But everything was him.

When the film finished we left in silence. Everyone left in silence, underwhelmed, chivvied by the theme ballad.

'That was mediocre,' Joshua said.

'It was. I sort of felt like crying. I'm embarrassed we sat through it. I'm just trying not to take it personally. Trying not to feel too affronted by the world.'

'I am taking it personally,' Joshua said, as we rode down on the escalator. 'That's kind of what I do. You know.'

A real wind was gusting about the car park. The tall lamp-posts – beginning to blink on, now – were quivering. We stood and looked around. Joshua swiped the hair out of his eyes and sucked air in through his teeth. His T-shirt fluttered.

'Oh, I suppose something biblical's going to happen,' I said.

Again, stepping through the tangled grass in the margin of the road, slipping on the pine straws, we walked as quickly as we could. I chatted on about the film for a while, but that died off. Doom was imminent. Pale thunderheads bloomed, whilst a colourless light kindled in the lower of the stacked clouds. The warm wind thudded against me; I leant into it, and it fell away. Twice there was a funny sprinkle of rain that lasted seconds, didn't catch. The hills rose black on either side now; and the river below us was a ribbon of snagged silk.

At the edge of downtown, waiters and waitresses were hurrying about the restaurant terraces, collecting tablecloths, walking stacks of chairs, winching in the canopies which were starting to swell and snap. A couple in one place glanced out at me; through a window framed with fairy lights shaped like gnarled baby chilli peppers, they glanced out and then looked back at each other.

On the street corners were the cabinets for the free-sheets, the What's On guides. I opened one, took out the last two papers, and held them over my head as I ran to catch up with Joshua. His slight figure was way up ahead of me now, moving towards the hotel.

Outside the Walgreen's there was a skinny blonde girl in a padded jacket sitting on the wall. She was rubbing her knuckles and shaking her head, muttering to herself, too. As I passed I heard, 'Smite them, Lord. Oh, smite them good.'

When I touched Joshua's back he turned, hunched his shoulders and put his hands over his head. He widened his eyes and stretched his mouth in a big O of fear. The rain was already roaring down.

14

Wringing my dress out over the short bathtub, I watched the black-flecked water swirl away.

Two flimsy plastic cups stood by the sink. They were printed with a blurred rendition of the hotel's sunrise logo. I took one out with me and filled it for Joshua, with the last of his whiskey. The cup was so light, I had to hold it steady while I poured. Joshua had stripped off, too, now. He was lying on the bed by the window, with his eyes closed, his hands steepled on his chest. He took the cup and held it there, on his sternum, watching me with one opened eye, as I sat up next to him and rubbed my wet legs. I rubbed his legs too, fluffed up the hair along his shinbones.

15

At first light, the rain was still falling, shushing the room. Joshua's breath was warm on my neck. We lay still like that, as the day began to glow mildly through the curtains, under the door.

'I guess I was pretty wasted last night,' Joshua said.

'Not especially. You were fine.'

'Well, I was sick, you know, after you went to sleep. I vomited, quite a bit.'

'Oh, no,' I said.

It occurred to me that I remembered something like that. Maybe I'd woken up and heard him, coughing and heaving.

'Do you remember switching beds?' he said.

I looked around. We had switched beds. The other one was in disarray, half-stripped, showing the pale green mattress ticking.

'No,' I said. 'Do I? No, I don't. Why did we?'

'I guess I was sweating pretty bad. That happens

sometimes. The sheets were kind of soaked, so . . .'

'Oh. Poor thing.'

'Yeah. Yesterday was fun, though.'

'Mmhmm.'

'That film sucked.'

'It did. I think it was the worst film I've ever watched.'

I twisted myself around to face him.

'Was it really?' he said.

And we looked at each other steadily.

16

That was how we looked at each other.

And then I followed him through the crowd, through the unfurling drabs of cigarette smoke, through the chit-chat. Finishing off my drink, I used my free hand to tug my hat and scarf back out from my bag. We went through a door marked Fire Exit, and then down a short, whitewashed corridor, made narrow by stacks of beer boxes and mop buckets. Joshua held the final door open.

It was a knife-sharp night. I still had my gin and tonic, and the bubbles bustled viciously in my nose as I took my final swig, put the glass down on a dirty lip of window ledge. Crossing the gritted car park side by side, Joshua and I both had our eyes screwed up against the icy wind. He hugged his sheepskin coat. When we reached the main road, as I stood searching in my bag for my bottle, he said, 'So, do you think it's *glamorous*, that I'm a divorcee?'

His smile then was tentative and also sly. Hapless and guileful. I just shrugged at him. I offered him some of my gin, but he had his own flask. He swigged away as we walked along. I swigged away too. In his hat and his stripy scarf, with his cheeks and nose flushed, he looked very fine, I thought.

'Well, I've never been married,' I said.

'You haven't?'

I shook my head.

'And, um, do you have a boyfriend around here?'

I shook my head at him again, and I grimaced.

He scratched at the back of his neck. His gloves were pale green, with white grips printed on the palms. There he was. Twenty-eight years old. The divorcee.

'So, what, is that a policy decision?' he said.

'I just want to write books,' I said. And then, 'I don't give a fuck about the rest of this set-up.'

And then I walked on, wondering about what I'd just said. I swigged some more of my burning lotion and I breathed out mist.

Buses kept rolling past us, all nearly empty now, just listing capsules of medical light. I started thinking, something like, Here's Manchester and here's Oxford Road. I like this man and he likes me. Something along those lines.

'So what's your novel about?' he said.

'I don't know,' I said. 'It's just existential.'

It was around then that there was that first soft collision. He stopped, stopped me, and leant in to kiss my cheek. We kept on walking afterwards. I turned to narrow my eyes at him. He was looking across at me, too, through the hair his hat flattened over his eyes.

I kept on kissing Joshua all through that night. I could hear the locked-out wind droning and crooning around my building, and I kept on, long into the cold grey morning. His mouth twisted and his body twisted. Sometimes his eyes were shut and sometimes they were open.

Afterwards, we lay facing each other, his legs pressed in against mine.

'Well. That's that out of the way,' he said. 'I guess.'

'Yes,' I said.

The lift was broken when we left. That lift that was always getting stuck. We had to walk down six floors, our footsteps' slow, syncopated clap-clapping flailing in echo, behind us and ahead of us.

17

Now Joshua's eyes were watering. There was his warm, soft, sleep-recent skin, the creased pillow-case lines printed on his cheek. He yawned into his hand, and said, 'I like *Tess*. You mentioned *Tess* the other day. And *Jude the Obscure*. You've read that, right?'

I nodded.

'If I was to have a favourite book, that might even be it,' he said.

I was yawning now, too.

'Poor old Jude,' I said. 'Those harpies took him down.'

I pulled the sheet back up over us, then, and the green, quilted cover, too, which lay gullied at the bottom of the bed. I pulled it up to under our chins. It was mid-afternoon. We'd come back up here after breakfast. I kicked my feet and shook my head. I turned over so my back was to Joshua and then twisted back around to face him again. He had his hands on my waist, sliding over my hips.

'You're kind of perky today,' he said. 'Flipping and flopping.'

'Yes,' I said. 'I am.'

He closed his eyes and smiled to himself.

'It's strange,' I said. 'I kept thinking of Jude Fawley when we were walking yesterday. I thought of him trudging from town to town.'

Joshua nodded. I put my finger on his fore-head for a moment.

'Incidentally, what's all this about?' I said, picking up the underpants that were on the bedside table. They were faded to a charcoal grey, and they were very small.

'Yeah,' he said, 'I guess those should go in the garbage. They're pretty stinky, right?'

'They're pretty skimpy. You're a man of extremes.'

'You think I should get some new ones?'

'I can't tell you what to do.'

He took the pants off me then, stretched them back on his thumb and sent them shooting towards the corner of the room. They lay there, draped on the lamp on the desk.

'Oh,' I said.

'So, anyway, how about you?' Joshua said. 'Would you have a favourite book? Dumb question, right?'

'No, it's not, except I'd have to say *The Great Gatsby*, and I wish it was something else.'

'Why's that?'

'Well. Because I hate it, that's why.'

'Okay. I guess I haven't read that one in a while.'

'Don't read it. It's unpleasant.'

Joshua nodded. He closed one eye.

'So, do you have a favourite book that you actually like?' he said.

'No.' I shook my head. 'Not really. All of them make me want to die, and then they won't even let me do that. There's always some goad. Some goading delusion that might secretly be real. If I picture Gatsby with his arms stretched out to Daisy's dock . . . It's a dreadful image. A person about to be scorned. Or maybe a person scorning their own life. Why would he do that to himself? But it's the same way a lot of us live, I think: fundamentally mistaken.'

'You think so?'

'No, I don't think so. That's my problem. I can see the evidence but I can't be convinced. I just — can't be convinced. It's like a strange dare. Maybe it's very nihilistic, maybe it's not. It's one or the other. It's like "The Imp of the Perverse".'

'Well,' Joshua said, 'I don't know about that. I guess I feel pretty overwhelmed a lot of the time, too, pretty depressed, but what keeps me going forward is at least a *mild* curiosity about how things might turn out. You know. This is my life. What's going to happen?'

He lifted his arms up and pressed his hands against the headboard as he yawned. His shoulders were plump and pale, but his forearms were tanned, and splashed with large, tea-coloured freckles. As he yawned, he moved his chin from side to side, and showed off his small, neat teeth. Then he rearranged himself on the pillow, and looked over at me. We were silent for a while, then, for maybe a minute, just breathing in and breathing out. Considering things.

Then I said, 'Whenever I get really down I go to see my doctor. It happens about once a year. This dizziness and fearfulness builds up, and I start to behave badly, drinking, trying to leave town, taking deadbeats home, generally being a menace, until finally I make an appointment. I arrive at the surgery in a highly strung state, but then, every time, the exact same thing happens. The exact same reversal. I tell the doctor that I've had enough, that I give in. Well, we don't like to just throw pills at a situation, she says. Tell me more specifically, what the problem is, why you feel this way? So I start to tell her. I describe my life, what it's made up of, what I do all day. I talk about my feelings and they sound so outlandish . . . I always start crying. I take the tissue she hands me and dab about with it, press it into my eyes. And then – quite suddenly, this happens every time – I realise that I haven't been looking at the doctor while I've been speaking. I've been looking at the carpet; out of the window at the bus stop; at her family photos on the mantelpiece . . . and she hasn't been looking at me either, and nothing I've said neces- sarily has any connection with the truth. And so I calm down quickly, and I just go home, without a prescription, with the same old counselling leaflet folded in my pocket, and destined to be forgotten.'

I looked back across at Joshua now. He said, 'You get a certain momentum going, I guess.'

'Yes,' I said, 'I suppose so. I do every now and then. Mostly I'm just sedated by terror at my own existence.'

'You are?'

'I don't know,' I said. 'I'm just talking. I'm just aggressively speculating as usual.'

I sat up in bed then and had a proper yawn, stretching my arms up into the cooler air. Sitting back against the padded headboard, I pushed all the covers right off me again, and crossed my legs in front of me. My head felt so thick, I'd been in bed so long, I'd entered some kind of an abstracted delirium.

'We have to get up,' I said, 'this is like *Huis Clos*. I'm turning into a soft furnishing.'

Joshua frowned to himself.

'I've never seen *Huis Clos*,' I said.

I got up and went to the bathroom, had another stretch in there, brushed my teeth twice. I drank three glasses of tap water and then took two cupfuls out with me. For a while Joshua and I both just sat up and drank our water, him still in bed, me on the chair by the desk. The water tasted sweet. I shivered a little as it went down. Then I spent some time picking at all the dried-up glue on my stomach. It was tight on my skin now; it looked like eczema.

The room we were in was large but low-ceilinged. Thickly bunched chintz curtains covered the front wall window, and dust swam in a screen of pale light coming in where they didn't quite meet. There was the In Case Of Fire poster, pinned to the door; the large air-conditioning unit chugging away. The carpet was the colour of pool-table felt.

Joshua had put his cup down.

'I came across a good word recently,' I said. 'You might like it: *aposematic*.'

'Oh. What's that?'

'Well – it's zoological. It refers to the markings and colours on animals or insects that serve to "warn or repel". I came up with this phrase, too: *the aposematic come-on*. I'm going to try and use it. I think it's what a lot of some people's behaviour constitutes. Like poking someone in the shoulder and saying, "Do you still like me?" Not caring about the answer particularly, asking the question again and again though. It works with some art, too, and with relation to God, ultimately, I suppose . . . It's tricky.'

Joshua winced.

'Oh? To God? Are you religious now?'

I shook my head. 'No, I don't mean that.'

Joshua looked at me with narrowed eyes. Sitting up with the duvet over his knees.

'Come back over here,' he said.

As I sat down next to him again, he poked a finger into my shoulder. He pressed it in hard a couple of times. His forearms were so densely freckled, they looked almost black in the dim light in there.

I said, 'I think the aposematic come-on is — it's what you do in the ultimate absence of anyone to talk to. It's a manifestation of aggressive hopelessness. Like maybe my books I wrote were just two stamped feet. Your plays, too. Or maybe they were the precise opposite of stamped feet. It's definitely one or the other. Do you ever think that?'

'I don't know,' Joshua said. 'I guess I've worried that there's at least an element of, um, *petulance*? maybe, in what I write.'

'Yes, that's the key word, isn't it?' I said. 'I said to my friend Jeane one time that all I was good for were petulant gestures against despair. She said, Lose the word petulant and that's fine. But I do feel petulant. When I try to fit certain ideas into my mind; when I try to acknowledge certain specifics of existence: it's like swallowing needles.'

I leant back against the headboard and breathed out. I'd actually been speaking the truth.

'So, your new book, how does that end?' Joshua said.

'Oh,' I said. 'Well, the heroine takes the love interest home, but they both just pass out drunk, and him while he's got two fingers still stuck up her dry cunt. When she wakes up they're gone, he's gone. And then – she decides to become a writer.'

'She does?'

'No. That's not what happens.'

'Oh.'

Joshua breathed out.

I said, 'I say these ugly things sometimes.'

'Yeah, well, that's okay.'

'Is it, though? I've seen how people end up.'

Joshua shook his head. He said, 'Christ, Natalie, you have to stop thinking about that. Although, you know, I've meant to ask you this before – is *cunt* like an okay word in England?'

'Yes, it's fine. I call everything a cunt ten times a day.'

'Because, over here, it's really bad.'

'Oh. Well –'

After a moment I pulled my knees up, crossed my arms. We were silent for a while.

'Well, don't worry about it,' Joshua said.

I nodded.

'I mean – come on, don't you think I'm sour?' he said.

'I suppose so. I suppose you are.'

I got back under the covers with him and we had another cuddle. I looked at his face, his drinktinctured face, blinking back at me. Under his right eye, burst vessels made a pink patch that never disappeared any more. I put my hand over his eyes for a moment, then pressed it down on his curling-up hair. Soon he started prodding at my boobs again.

'What's this?' he said, shaking his head. 'Looks like – double trouble.'

Some more time passed. We'd moved the pillows and were lying the other way up in the bed, facing the gilt-framed Smoky Mountain scene over the headboard, talking again. We were talking about our childhoods.

'If I remember myself as a kid,' Joshua said, 'I was *so* laid back. It was hilarious. I was a little stoner at age, like, eight. I guess 'cause I was the youngest – I'm the youngest by seven years – and I was unexpected, my parents must have really had it with constant supervision. I could pretty much please myself, and I liked to take it easy. My older brothers had all the pressure off Dad – they're still mad at me about that, I think. But I was just like everyone's little pet. My Mom would always say that I would end up a beach bum. Because I liked to just lay out in the back yard, with a can of soda and a comic book, for, you know, days on end? I even had a little tank top that said "Beach Bum" across it.'

'Good God.'

'Ya, it's pretty cute, I know. It is. I have photos.'

'I bet you do.'

Joshua shrugged and narrowed his eyes at me, and then he squeezed me against him, hard until I could barely breathe. I felt my skin slide over my ribs, like when you pick up a cat. Joshua made a low growling noise. I said, 'Stop it, ouch,' and closed my eyes, smiling to myself, quite happy now. When he let me go I lay on my back.

'Oh. That was good,' I said.

Joshua scratched the top of his chest and grinned for a second. The lines gathered around his eyes. Thin lines that ticked up into his temples.

'God, I loved being a boy,' he said. 'Playing all day, hanging out. I had this best friend, Merritt, and we would put all our toys together, and his sister's toys, and it'd be, well Chewbacca's ill here, in Barbie's house, and now there's a blizzard, and we need to get this ambulance through the snow . . .'

'Collaboration. Interesting.'

'Yeah. I still like toys, actually. I used to like playing with all my nieces and nephews, buying them birthday gifts and what not. I have a lot of nice toys in my apartment, too. Not like gadgets, I mean, old-fashioned, well-made toys. I have this wooden fire truck in my living room. If I ever have kids it'll be so great.'

'This is interesting. I wouldn't have guessed that about you. I wouldn't know how to behave around children, myself. I haven't met any since school. If I met an eight-year-old now, I can see myself sitting somewhere with it, and us both swinging our legs, and me telling it how confused I am in my personal life and my creative existence. Even when I was a kid, though, I never liked toys. I had a chemistry set, I had a globe I used to listlessly spin, lots of books.'

'Well, you would strike me as someone who was just wanting to know about the world, right?'

'You think so? Well, maybe that was it,' I said. 'I used to learn capital cities, the Greek alphabet. I had a broad scope. I wasn't lonely in a despairing way so much as resigned to a period of loneliness. I still am, actually. It's called my lifespan.'

'Oh. Really?'

'I don't know. That just occurred to me. Sometimes I think loneliness is in the past, but it always comes back.

'Anyway. I was saying, I didn't like toys. But when I was very young I did like doing craft projects with my Mum, making pictures, felt animals, badges, that kind of thing.

'And later on, when I was a teenager, I used to skive off school a lot, to lie on the settee with a cushion on my face and just – explore the possibilities of my own brain. I couldn't go out in case I got seen, so I just lay there, with the curtains closed, having these concentrated day-dreams. Damn it, this is no good, I'm starting to feel sad again.'

'Don't feel sad,' Joshua said.

'Remembering is a kind of pornography, don't you find?'

'I guess. It can be.'

'It seems to be the way my mind's calibrated, anyway. Maybe it's my line of work. I'll have to give that some thought. I like hearing about you, though. That's different. You should keep going. I used to think this information was too arcane to ask about. But I do want to know. What comes after the Beach Bum years?'

'Oh. Okay. Well, I guess in high school I just got more and more deadpan, you know, in that slightly ridiculous way that teenagers do? I was so sardonic. I'm surprised I didn't get beat up on more than I did. I always had to draw atten-tion to myself. It was pathological. I mean, I streaked the prom. Nudity was a big part of my life back then.'

'I see. Were you always pressing your bottom against cold glass?'

'I did like to do that. And then at college, drama students, they're really the worst. My friends anyway. Everything I wrote back then seemed to involve me getting buck-naked. In my final show, I was supposed to be urinating in a bucket while I did my monologue, but I guess due to nerves, I couldn't, so I was just standing there, you know, making this speech, holding my dick.'

'And you don't want to act again?'

'No. I never did, really. Or, if I did, I got over it pretty fast. I always just wanted to write. More and more that's how I want to spend my time.'

'I like writing,' I said. 'I like it for about fifteen minutes, on aggregate, every two years.'

'Oh. You don't enjoy it?'

'Well, it's like I say, but if I didn't do it, what would there be? That's the point. I even miss it now, and it's only been a couple of days. Not doing it feels like a space walk. But – now we're really lying here, and maybe it's the same thing, in a way, trying to marshal this . . . ephemera . . .'

'I don't know about that,' Joshua said. 'Are you calling me ephemera?'

'I hate to break it to you.'

'Are you saying you want to marshal my ephemera?' he said.

I considered this.

'I don't know,' I said. 'Maybe we could marshal each other's. We could take turns. Good God. I don't like this conversation. Let's change the subject.'

Joshua lay back on the pillow looking at me in an insolent way.

I said, 'Anyway. Hands off. So. All these brothers you've got, do you see them much?'

He shook his head.

'No, not really. I stopped going home, for Thanksgiving, Christmas. I haven't been back in maybe three years? My whole family is kind of screwed, actually. My Dad, he's such a languid fascist these days. My Mom is like – a hologram. I don't think those two have had a conversation in a decade. And every one of my brothers is hopelessly dependent on something. For most of them it's religion, for the rest it's alcohol, or else . . . sci-fi. They all have families now, though, and good jobs, I guess, they're all corporate lawyers, and so they talk to me like I'm a retard or something, you know, *And how's the artist?* That irritates me but, whatever.

'When I was younger I really used to get on with my oldest brother, Gabe. I used to think he was so much fun, but as it turns out, he's insane. He's been institutionalised a number of times, now. It's pretty sad, actually. But despite that, I still get to be the black sheep of the family. My aunts are the worst about that. They've all taken to calling and leaving messages saying how upset Mom is that I don't go home, how she's not well . . . But the idea of going back makes me so exhausted. And I tend to think, you know, not one of them ever treated me like a grown-up, why should I have to act like one now? Right?'

'I don't know. I don't know what that means. Are you being serious?'

'I don't know. I'm just talking. This subject brings me down. Another thing I get to feel guilty about, you know?'

He took his hand from my waist then and pushed his hair back out of his face.

'Well,' I said, 'guilt's not nice to live with. But you can only do what you're going to do, can't you? We can't help the people we are. I mean, I was a tyrant to my parents. When they were dying and I was going to live. I was insatiable. It's difficult to think about, but I don't feel guilty. When I watched Dad die, it was sad, it was very . . . *unsettling*, but even then I knew it was for the best. I wouldn't have been good at dealing with him grabbing at me all my life. And he would have done, you know. I remember he was always telling me how he used to put head-phones on my Mum's bump to play me his records. He was so pleased with himself about that, but it made me furious every time he told me, like, Christ, couldn't you ever leave me alone? Couldn't you ever keep your hands off? I was in the womb, for God's sake!'

Joshua was laughing. His eyes were wide.

'Well, I was inchoate,' I said. 'It's a bit much. I sound callous, I know, but it's how I feel, so . . . I'm just telling you. I mean, speaking of emotional pornography, I used to picture my Mum, in her seventies clothes, sat on the settee with those big, old-style headphones on her bump. I can see exactly the look she would have had on her face too, this dreadful patient waiting for time to pass, being held hostage by that volatile bore, and nothing she could do about it. It wasn't fair, what happened to her . . . But it isn't fair what happens to any of us, I suppose. Listen, did you ever read this book *The Dead Father*, by Donald Barthelme?'

Joshua shook his head.

'It sums the situation up,' I said, 'quite accurately. That's Dads, I think, sadly, overbearing, ineffectual, exercising their infantile tyrannies until everyone's bored and tired out. It is tragic. It's terrifying. But they have to go. When Mum died, that was different, much more frightening. I'm glad she was cremated, at least. If I had to think of her body, boxed-up, underground – that might be too much.'

Joshua took his arm from around me again then, and he held it in the air, spread his fingers and closed one eye. He looked back at me. 'Well, I don't think my Mom's going to *die* anytime soon,' he said. 'But it is on my mind.'

I said, 'Well, they were dropping like flies when I was growing up.'

Joshua raised his eyebrows.

I rubbed my eyes and then I went on. 'I read a description of F. Scott Fitzgerald's dead body once,' I said, 'They disinterred him to re-bury him next to Zelda, and one of the gravedigger people gave an account. He'd been dead thirty years then, I think, and he and Zelda had been separated for a while before he died, but their daughter petitioned the Catholic Church to let them be buried together. So I read this description. His coffin had a glass viewing panel, and they saw his tight yellow skin, dry yellow hair, sunken eye sockets, Princeton tie: F. Scott Fitzgerald. Dead.'

Joshua squinted at the wall behind me.

'Yeah. That's kind of weird,' he said.

We were both silent for a while.

And then he went on. 'It's funny, though, you know, talking about Scott and Zelda. Maybe they did belong together like that. I think what I've come to realise, is that marriage does make you family. I didn't consider it at the time, when I got married, but it's true. Later on, and even more so, actually, as the years go by, I realise that my ex-wife and I – it can't be undone.'

'Really?'

'Yeah. You know, I think you'd be surprised if you ever met her. She's – I don't know.'

He kept looking straight ahead, then; kept on looking like a man thinking about his ex-wife. Which didn't mean he wasn't, of course. In fact, I'm sure that's exactly what he was doing. So glum. I found it soothing though, in a way. I always had.

His body was nice and warm. I lifted his left arm up and put my head down there, with my face in his armpit. I took a deep breath and held tight.

18

It was no good, though. It was no good. I was wide awake and restless, long after Joshua's eyes had closed, and he'd turned to face me, and his breathing had deepened. I wriggled against him a bit, but he didn't come back to life. I found his hand and held it, and he clicked his tongue then, but he didn't squeeze my hand in reply. The curtain-filtered light was irritating. My stomach kept growling. I had to get up. Rolling over, I swung my feet onto the carpet; I got dressed quietly, and finally found my key card by the sink. Joshua was still asleep when I left, lying face down, with one hand under his head. I left him with the sheet pulled off his smooth bare back.

Emerging from that fake night into the late afternoon, I was glad of the cool, fresh wind; the chlorine smell, and the mulchy rainwater smell. A skinny man in shorts and a Chicago Bulls T-shirt was coming out of the room next door and we nodded hello. He walked off towards the lift, his hands shoved deep into his pockets. I went the other way, and waited, leaning on the gallery rail.

Asheville was still vividly wet. The roads ran slick into the hills. Long reefs of cloud shadowed the crumpled landscape. Down in the pool, standing chest-deep in the water, was a woman wearing rubber gloves with her swimsuit. She stood and shook, as sometimes with the sponge in her right hand and sometimes with the scouring pad in her left, she kept rubbing at the mossy paint above the water-line. When she'd finished one spot she moved on, wading.

The vending machine by the lift held up a solitary bag of trail mix and a short queue of Babe Ruth bars. I was considering it, turning over the thin coins in my pocket. Instead, I pressed the Down button again, and then took the stairs instead. The walls in the stairwell were mapped by old grouting, pale scrapes of glue.

Out on Patton Avenue, some kids were sitting on a low wall opposite the record shop: a girl and three younger boys, all with black hair swept across their ardent faces. I turned onto another street, lined with canopied restaurants, where spruced-up families were spilling from huge cars, massing on the pavement, before setting out for dinner.

I couldn't work out, amongst all this evening bustle, what it was that was absent, and that made the town feel so quiet and still. I kept on walking, and soon I found myself in the grounds of a college, on a damp lawn in a quiet quadrangle. Through one open window I saw an office with bookshelves, somebody's den; there was an architect's lamp on in there, and a radio, a phone-in show. There was a postcard of W. H. Auden's cracked face tacked up on a corkboard.

'Just a tonic water, please. Cheers.'

The drink was set down on a green napkin. It came with a plastic stirrer and a brisk smile. This place wasn't too busy, it was hopsy-smelling, gently lit, and I felt okay, sitting up on a stool, prodding the ice cubes about in my glass. I hadn't been in a bar in a year, that was the thing.

The girl who'd served me was leaning forward on the counter. Her frayed blonde curls fell to her shoulders. Another girl, also in the uniform black T-shirt gone grey, and shiny black trousers, came over and stood opposite her. Her back said, *O'Connor's Taproom*. Both frowned up at the dusty cuckoo clock above the Budweiser fridge, which seemed to still say 8.25.

'Well, I saw that coming,' the redhead said.

'We always do, though,' said the blonde, screwing up her face, looking tired, baffled with tiredness.

'We always do.'

She rubbed her eyes with a bony hand. Several silver rings glinted there.

'I bet when the world ends we'll all be like, *I knew it,*' she said.

Towards the back of the room, the chairs and tables gave way to a less inviting space, a maze of unlit, empty booths. A man in chef's check trousers and a white vest was moving about there, clearing up. His dishrag wagged in the gloom.

The two girls at the bar watched him and shook their heads.

And the closer he came, the older he looked, with his blue-black quiff and grizzled, mousy sideburns. He came towards us, and as he passed her, he gave the blonde girl's bottom a pat. He pinched up his face then, braced himself for her reaction.

'He *really* needs to stop doing that,' she said finally.

'Amy says, No more ass touching,' the other girl called out.

Pausing in the kitchen doorway, the man turned around, rested his chin on top of the menus he was carrying. Behind him was all strip-lit, brushed steel, disinfectant and grease.

'Well, you can't prevent it if it happens, can you?' he said. 'That's like saying, No more rain.'

'I swear to God,' the blonde girl said, 'sometimes they look at you and it's like a big old neon check mark appears over your head. Yeah, well done, mister, you got me drunk.'

The taller girl nodded.

'What we need is a tranquilliser gun,' she said. 'Or maybe a cattle prod? You know what a cattle prod does, don't you? It delivers a shock.'

After that they stood in silence for a while. A bored silence overtook them both.

And then the blonde girl went on: 'Last year back in New York, though. That was the worst. I had a seminar but I couldn't face it. So I was just roaming around Washington Square. This guy asked me for directions, to the library, anyways, next thing you know, we're in a bar, and next thing you know, we're doing it on the bathroom floor, and in the men's room, too. He was swearing at me in Portuguese, calling me a whore. I mean, what is the point of that? I was lying there wondering, Why am

I here, underneath this Portuguese whore-caller?'

Each time the door opened, those girls looked up, and certain of the customers too; heads lifted and dropped. The man next to me, with smoke bursting from his coughing mouth – small blue clouds that unravelled as they faded – he sat there and looked at the door. And so I sat, my eyes moving from the small, muted TV, to those girls, to the door, and still knocking my ice cubes about, getting through the plastic basket of pistachio nuts that had been placed in front of me. I felt slightly uneasy that I'd left Joshua. I thought of him in our dark room, breathing in and breathing out. I closed my eyes, and for a while I just did the same.

The TV was showing rolling local news. Weather symbols jerked over a low-resolution map: digital clouds stuttered towards Atlanta.

Each time the headlines began again, it was with the same photograph, of a fluffy-haired middle-aged woman, wearing a peach bridesmaid's dress. It flashed up again now, followed by a more recent mug-shot, of a man with salt-and-pepper hair scraped back from a blank, lipless face. The screen was so busy. Somewhere the words FORMER LOVER seemed to scroll by, and next, in front of a gurney with straps, a young reporter explained the procedure for tonight. Death being a matter of logistics.

North Carolina has the death penalty. I hadn't known that. But then I didn't know much about the country I was in, did I? It was enormous in scale, fraudulent by nature. You had to be able to drive. That was where I'd put myself, though. I prised open the shell of another nut, looked around the room. And there was no one I could talk to in there, any more than I could have phoned Jeane up. It wasn't possible.

That chef character was out and about again soon enough; leaning against the wall, talking to the girls. I looked at him and thought, Well, I know you, anyway, with your deadpan face, with your face like an old apple that someone took a bite out of and then left.

Jeane used to work in a bar. She did six shifts a week in a tiny flock-wallpapered corridor on Portland Street. The Crown. A place where leftovers went to pick at each other. I sometimes used to meet Jeane down there, at the end of the night. What a sight that was; her boss, gimlet-eyed in his corner, lifting his little boot-clad feet up so she could mop.

'We have fun here, don't we?' he used to say.

'Party party party. Laughing our heads off all day long.'

And his girlfriend, that drear spectre, eyes like thumb holes in grey clay, as she leant over to have him light her bent cigarette. The bouncer would stand, arms folded, swirling his head around on his huge neck. There were brown-and-orange beer signs and balding upholstery. That was the Crown. The tin hat. I remember going with Jeane down to the basement office there, one night after she'd cashed up.

'Dave's been worried,' she said – Dave was her boss – 'because last week he found out he'd caught chlamydia – from one of those girls he takes home. And he and Jeni are trying for a baby, so he had no choice but to tell her. He decided the best way around it was to say he didn't sleep with anyone else, he just got a blow job when he was drunk.'

'And how did that go down?'

'Okay, I think.' Jeane said. 'She's just bought him a PlayStation 2 for Valentine's Day.'

'That's not even a good story,' I said.

'I know. I know it's not. My brain is empty.'

That office was a narrow, crypt-cold room, lit by two caged wall lights. Battered filing cabinets stood amongst bicycle frames and broken chairs. Cobwebs hammocked cringing spider-skins, and a huge old computer huffed and churned. I was so bored that night I picked one of the chairs up and started swinging it at the wall. I smashed it hard against the whitewashed, mould-splashed bricks, until the greasy wood splintered and the old nails bent. Jeane took it off me when my arms got tired. She started swinging it about, too, and baring her little teeth and stamping.

When she stopped, she shook her head, and said, 'Actually, why shouldn't you give someone a PlayStation when they've given you chlamydia? It's fine. Why should actions and reactions match? I mean, how can they, anyway? How could they ever do that?'

Jeane's other half, Mick, used to drink in the Temple. Sometimes I went and found him there, installed with the rest of the guzzling set. At this point, his take on the world was only like white noise, too.

'*Trivia, Natalie!*' he'd say. 'You were pissed. Don't worry about it. If I looked through a telescope I'd still see you and him, just like if you looked through a telescope you'd see me and Jeane. Facts are facts, come on!'

Facts are facts. Because for every one of us

who suspects there's something wrong with their dreams, there are matter-of-fact visionaries, like him.

Mick's laugh was a rat-a-tat cackle that snapped his head right back, like garrotting wire might, while he gripped the edge of the bar and his stool wobbled underneath him, half-pirouetted and then crashed down again. You could have said he had 'mobile features', except that you never saw them move. His expression simply changed, dramatically and often. He was incredulous, overwhelmed, scornful, *delighted*. A face like a slideshow. And my face would mirror his when we were talking to each other. That was an effect he had.

I went to see him after Joshua didn't show up last year. My final night out, when I really did feel I was being processed by the vortex; when I'd drunk every bottle I'd bought for me and him, and all of my insides were like pulped leather, and my face was hot and swollen.

'This is the end,' I said. 'Witness this: I'm making myself a chrysalis out of dried vomit.'

'Oh, well, listen,' Mick said, 'we're *all* at a transitional phase in our lives, Natalie. All that is solid melts into air: Karl Marx. We're in flux. Fluxed up!'

And he was right. And so there were always all these breathless activities: the slipshod getaways; the mugging and expounding; the scab-picking literature I'd written as each new liturgy of exhilaration became just *brick wall brick wall brick wall . . .*

When the barmaid came over again and took my glass I said, 'Yes. Yes, please,' to another tonic water.

'And y'all want ice and lemon in that?' she said.

'Yes, please. Why not?'

19

An elderly couple were sitting in the Days Inn lobby, squashed together, uncomfortably close, on the small leather sofa by the souvenir cabinet. When I pushed open the door they glared up at me so forlornly.

'Any minute now,' said the night clerk.

He was still leafing through his newspaper. He had both his elbows on the reception desk, and was just batting the pages back and forth. There'd always been easy-listening playing down there before: minot-key muzak, 'Moon River' on a kazoo, late Sinatra maybe, but now it was silent save for those turning pages.

With half of the room cordoned off, breakfast had been relegated to a trestle table by the lift. On the waxed paper tablecloth were three bronze plastic coffee flasks and a stack of polystyrene cups so tall it leant over like a palm-tree trunk. Yesterday's dried-out rolls shared a basket with several large, knuckly, red apples. There was a plastic tub of punishing-looking cereal, too: a tombola with no prizes. I put my hand on one of the coffee flasks.

'Is this still hot, then?' I asked the man at the desk.

'Yes, it should be. We have hot coffee twenty-four hours a day. There's no milk there right now, but I can get you some if you hold on for *just* a minute.'

'No, that's okay, I don't take milk. Thank you.'

I held down the button and my cup filled with smoking silt. The old woman on the settee had craned her neck around to watch me.

I took an apple, next, put it in my bag for later, and then one for Joshua, too. The muffins were stale, but I took one anyway, and leant back on the table, and tore it up in its case. I was poking them into my coffee, these tough little rinds of sponge, before eating them.

The old man cleared his throat.

'What's all this "No Locals" then? You don't like the locals here?' he said. He was chuckling to himself.

Turning to look at the sign, the desk clerk smiled and then leant back on his heels.

'Well, no,' he said. 'Ah — that would just be for the local people who maybe mistook this hotel for a — brothel?' he said. 'We hung that sign to really try and discourage that misunderstanding.'

'Oh,' said the old man. 'Oh. I see. I get you.'

He smiled weakly over at his wife, as he sank back into the sofa. She looked dully across at the entrance. They both of them had tufty white hair, dyed in places in a mixture of cat's tummy colours: amber and yellow and chestnut brown.

Instead of going straight upstairs, I took my drink out onto the patio. I sat down next to the lit-up pool, cross-legged on the brushed concrete. There was only the chirruping of insects out there, the low hum of the generator. Banked up in front of me were four floors of closed curtains and TV light. The waning moon just touched the hotel roof.

When I'd finished off my coffee I swilled the bloated crumbs around in the dregs.

The water looked so cool. I leant forward and dipped one hand in, then both hands. The water-line grazed up my wrists, and I saw my blanched hands hanging there, spreading and clutching.

20

The clock on the TV said 01.40. Red numbers glowing in the dark. And the covers were pushed off both of the beds, now — they were heaped on the floor. I stepped around them. The same thing had happened again, then. Was he in the bathroom? I crouched down to look. There was a faint line of light down there. The fan was quietly rattling.

On the nearest bed, the sheet was soaked through, and the pillow, too, was dented and soaked. The bed we'd abandoned last night hadn't dried off either. I was pressing on the mattress, screwing up my face, when the bathroom door opened. Joshua stood there in the whirring light, blinking down at himself. He was rubbing his chest with a hand towel. His skin glistened and his hair looked raggy, matted.

'Oh. You're back,' he said.

He grimaced, set his jaw, as he lifted his legs up one by one and rubbed them down.

'What's all this? Are you okay?'

'Don't! Your hands are cold! Sorry. Your hands . . .'

'Sorry.'

He sucked in some air and blew it carefully out, keeping his eyes wide.

'I'm not ill. This happens sometimes. I gotta take these off.'

He tugged his soppy white pants off and put them in the sink, then kept rubbing himself with that little towel. He was avoiding looking at me, frowning down at the floor.

'I can't get back in that bed,' he said.

'Well, no, they're both quite clammy now. We need more beds. You should sit down.'

He didn't though. He turned the bathroom light off and then just stood up in the far corner, with his shoulders pinched forward, and shuddering.

'Do you want a blanket?'

He shook his head.

'I'm burning up here.'

The sheets on last night's bed smelt like old potato peelings. I balled them up and put them by the door.

Eventually I managed to flip the mattress over, and then we lay under the two dry blankets, him

128

behind me, clutching my shoulders. The blankets were itchy. I could feel Joshua's belly pressed onto my back, the hair on it all slimy with sweat.

'This is bad,' he said. 'This is really bad.'

'Oh, Joshua,' I said, 'you poor, sick, playwright.'

'Have I been drinking too much?' he said. 'Or not enough?'

I felt his chin press down: his stubble rub against my neck.

'I wanted to have a drink tonight,' I said. 'I was walking around town feeling like a drained lake.'

There was a pause. 'You didn't, though?' he said.

'No,' I said, 'the idea seemed like drudgery in the end. I thought I'd hold off. I sat in a bar for a while, that's all.'

'Well, I just woke up and you'd gone.'

'I know. I'm sorry. I should have left a note. Hold onto me now.'

I drew my legs up and he did the same behind me. His tickly thighs, scalding hot, pressed against the back of mine as he shuddered and shivered and hissed.

21

Before coming away here, the last place I'd seen Joshua was Leeds city centre, just some paved precinct between a Café Rouge and an HSBC Bank. We'd said goodbye there – had a hard hug through our winter coats – one twilit lunch hour just over two years ago.

The West Yorkshire Playhouse were putting on a new play of his; that's why he was in the country, to give notes on the rehearsals. On the night he arrived he called me, from his room in the Holiday Inn Express. He couldn't sleep, he said, 'And this TV doesn't work.' I could picture him pointing the remote as we spoke, aiming it upwards.

I went to meet him the next afternoon.

Tired commuters filled the train, their scuffed briefcases on their laps, and shoppers with their bags between their feet, and no one with enough elbow room to take their coats off. I edged up the aisle, and managed to get a seat at Stockport. I leant on the window and watched the sky darken, the low sun flickering through the moss-smeared saplings that fenced the embankment. Soon there were only misty frosted fields and the night-glow of gritstone Pennine towns.

Reluctant to relax into the iciness, I held my body braced as I hurried down the station approach. I walked stiffly, trying to resist the conciliatory shudder. Signposts led me along the main shopping street, still fixed up with dead Christmas lights, and then down a narrow alley, where a run of empty, glass-fronted bars gave way to a cobbled slope, and then a car park.

From there I saw the Playhouse, a yellow-brick building lit up against the clear black sky. I stopped for a moment when I saw it, and had another drink.

In the foyer, making an effort to breathe normally again, I walked around, rubbing my hands together. They felt so dry and cold. Like cold rubber. I took deep breaths and shook them.

There didn't seem to be anybody about who I could ask about Joshua. The ticket office was shut up. I could hear voices from the café area . . .

I was heading up there, when, from around a corner, an old man in blue overalls appeared. He was walking quite slowly, tugging the bulbous body of an industrial vacuum cleaner behind him. Stopping a few feet into the lobby, he switched his machine on, pressing a button with his booted foot, and started to shunt the nozzle about. I walked over to him.

'Do you know where the rehearsals are happening?' I said.

He squinted at me, deaf beneath the hoover's droning. He switched it off again.

'What's that, love?' he said.

'I'm looking for the rehearsals?'

'Can't help you there, love,' he said.

The droning began again.

I walked up the stairs to the café. On the far side of that room I saw some of the bar staff waiting to start, young people in white shirts and green waistcoats. They'd taken the chairs down off one of the tables and were all sitting around there, holding steaming vending-machine cups, leaning back in their seats. Someone who'd come in behind me went over and joined them. A girl called to him: ' 'Allo, 'aircut.'

' 'Allo, trouble,' he said, and then turning back to me: 'Not open yet, love.'

'Yeah,' I said. 'I'm just looking for my friend, actually. He's working around here somewhere. Rehearsing? Where would that be?'

The boy cocked his head, but didn't answer me. He was thinking.

I put my hands back in my coat pockets and looked around.

'Oh,' the boy said. 'Hold on. Here's someone who'll know.'

A woman with curly hair and glasses had appeared from another door. She did look official. I asked her, and she smiled absently at me, said, 'Joshua. Yes,' and told me to go straight through to the studio, that's where everyone was.

'Thank you,' I said.

And I went where she'd pointed, down the short flight of stairs, through a set of heavy fire doors. There was a Ladies' room there and I went in to fix myself up. My hair was all whipped about and my nose was pink. I rubbed make-up onto my nose and cheeks, under my eyes. I had another drink in there, too, and then leant back on the sinks and waited, watching the minutes pass on the clock on my phone. My heart was beating quite purposefully.

★

On stage, on a single bed, a young couple were sitting together. They looked up as I came in, pulling the auditorium door slowly shut behind me. They looked up and then down again. I stayed where I was; against the back wall. I stood very still in the close and quiet darkness.

After a moment, the man spoke. He was using a strange American accent.

'*Um,*' he said, squinting one eye up, '*so, is that your favourite dress?*'

The girl touched her collarbone and looked down at herself. Currently she was wearing a festive red jumper and jeans tucked into boots.

'*Oh, no,*' she said (she was English, northern), '*I just always wear it.*'

'*Well, I guess this is my favourite shirt.*'

'*Is it? It is nice.*'

'*My ex-wife took my favourite favourite shirt, though. When she went back to Denver? She took her stuff, and she took my sky-blue shirt. I thought that was pretty mean. I mean, what could she want with it?*'

The girl looked up at him then, quite sharply, and he scratched his forehead, squinted again, before coughing and checking the floppy, stapled script that was balanced on his knees.

134

Now that my eyes had adjusted, I looked around the room again, down at the shadowed stalls. And there was Joshua. There he was after all. I walked down the aisle towards him. He'd been sunk very low in his seat; he was sitting up straighter now. The couple on stage were watching me, and finally he turned around to see what they were looking at.

'Oh,' he said, 'hey,' and he stood up, and bent down to put his coffee cup on the floor.

He edged out into the aisle. His hair was longer. A strand went in my mouth when he gave me a hug.

In the over-lit theatre bar, we sat in a corner, in our uncomfortable chairs. Joshua had a half-bottle in the pocket of his sheepskin coat, and he was sharing the last of it with me now that we'd finished mine off. His play was called *Bright Girl Wanted, Saturdays*. I was writing another book then, too. I was writing a book called *Time is Like a Lump*. I was telling Joshua all about it when a man came over to say hello.

'Hey,' Joshua said, looking up. 'Natalie, this is Bill, he's directing the play. And this is Natalie, that, um, author I was telling you about.'

'Hi there,' I said.

Bill looked to be in his early forties. He had a baffled, bristly face. He was dressed something like a hill walker, in a purple zip-up fleece, and with a green bobble hat on the back of his head.

'Nice to meet you,' he said. 'Hello! And you're from here, is that right?'

'Well, I'm from Manchester,' I said, and then I went on, for no clear reason, 'My great-grandad came from nearby, though. He was chauffeur to the Lord Mayor of Rotherham and he lived to be a hundred and four. Harriet Harman kept sending him telegrams.'

Bill nodded sagely. He seemed nice but I didn't want him to sit down with us. We were in our own dimension, currently.

'I grew up in Rotherham,' he said, one hand in his pocket, one scratching his chin. 'Never went back. Last thing my father said to me, You'll not go to art school! You'll not go to art school in that duffel coat! Ha! Should have listened to *Pater*, I could have been Chancellor of the Exchequer by now!'

I giggled. Joshua looked candidly bored in that way he was good at.

'So. Two writers!' Bill said. 'Okay for drinks?'

'Another whiskey would be *great*,' said Joshua,

and he reached down very slowly to get his wallet from his coat. Bill shook his head.

'Put that away,' he said. He looked at me. 'Drink?' he said, nodding.

'Can I get a gin with just a tiny bit of tonic please,' I said.

'Mother's ruin!' he said. He went off towards the bar, but soon veered off to chat to the actors.

'You're a brat, Joshua,' I said.

'Yeah. I should talk to him,' he said. 'I guess. It's kind of a drag, but, first day here and every-thing. I'm sorry. I meant to ask before, actually, will you be able to get back tonight?'

'Yes, no problem; the trains run until three.'

He nodded.

'Okay.'

Bill was coming back with our drinks. I saw his bobble hat approaching and nudged Joshua. They were doubles too, what he brought us, but still each time he went outside for a smoke, either Joshua or I went to the bar and got two shots, which we got rid of before he came back. We were horrible. We were quite horrible that night.

When Bill's taxi arrived to take him home, we both watched him trot down the stairs. Joshua kind of smiled down at his drink.

'I don't think he likes my play,' he said. 'I don't think he wants to direct it.'

'No? That's not good.'

Joshua shrugged.

'Just a few things he said. I don't know. Fuck him, right? So, I'm guessing there are no trains back to Manchester now,' he said.

'Well, I don't know,' I said.

Joshua was leaning back in his seat, looking up through his hair. He had his grey cardigan on, a checked shirt with the pocket torn off. His hat was on the table.

'Anyway, it's good to see you,' he said. 'You look good. I never know what you're going to look like.'

'I see.'

'You know what I mean. Do you like my play?'

'I do,' I said. 'It seemed to be quite – pointlessly tender.'

He shrugged his shoulders at that, and then he stood up, and had a stretch, before taking my hand and pulling me up too. We walked arm in arm in the general direction of the door.

Back at the hotel, his gloved hands were in fists, pressed on my back as I was pressed up against the lift mirror. His mouth was sour. His skin was icy. I felt the pin spikes of hair on his icy neck. After the kissing, he exhaled roughly, leant down heavily on my shoulder.

We were together for three days, then. While he was working I wandered round town. I went to the pictures, spent hours in various clattering cafés, writing in my notebook, pouring my gin into mugs and paper cups. At night we got drunk in the bar, then back in his room.

I remember the walk from the theatre to the hotel each night, stumbling through the chip-shop, taxi-queue alleyways as though we were in a three-legged race, heads drooping, legs buckling; me making my usual speeches, telling him what I'd read or written, bad things I'd done. I quoted Denis Johnson and called everything a cunt. All that fuming hyperbole in the icy night air.

And he was at it, too; back in that small room. One night he solemnly took my hand.

'You know, I cheated on every girlfriend that I ever had,' he said. 'Every one of 'em.'

His eyes pooled with such grave and gorgeous contrition. He pressed my hand against his rough face.

'I would never cheat on you,' he said.

I remember narrowing my eyes at him, lying on the pillows in a scalding heap, waiting to not be conscious. And his lined and blotchy face, blinking slowly back at me. There was nothing we could do. Momentum was lacking.

We didn't talk much in the mornings. The hour between waking up and going out was a time to be got through. He would fill a two-litre Volvic bottle from the bathroom tap, and bring it back to bed. Sitting with his knees bent up in front of him, he'd drink half of the misty water down, in a chain of laborious gulps, before passing it over to me.

And then, on the last day, as he was packing his rucksack, kneeling to push his striped wash bag down into the shirts and shorts, he said, 'But what would –'

He coughed, looked surprised, and clapped his hand on his sternum. 'Pardon me,' he said. His baritone was restored. 'I mean – what would you and I *do*, Natalie?'

'In what way?'

'I mean, if you and I were together, what would we do?'

'I haven't thought about that. What do you think?'

He frowned to himself, and then looked over at me quite blankly – it seemed like an accidental glance – before he stood and started to button up his shirt, looking down with one eye closed.

'Okay,' I said. 'Okay. Well, how about this – I can't see myself procreating and so we'd just have to be ourselves. That's my answer. Does that sound horrifying enough?'

In the thin mirror on the back of the wardrobe door, I was watching myself say these things.

Joshua didn't reply. Drawing the curtains, pushing aside the stiff nets, he looked out of the window, and up at the weather, the soiled white sky. His face was washed with that frigid light. When he turned around he said, 'I guess I'm just – I'm – a practical person?'

I didn't feel good. In the same way that coldness or drunkenness numbs your fingers first, and your lips, and works outwards, I felt this unreality begin to inhabit me. In that suspended room. I blinked my dried-out eyes.

My dress was on the floor. I picked it up and then sat down with it, held it in my lap. I watched Joshua as he pulled his trousers up: there were his slim shoulders in green check; the curls of hair flattened on the back of his head.

I said, 'Or how about this: it's an early winter's morning like this one, but we've kept the curtains closed, and we're both sat up in bed writing on our laptops, and our faces are lit up by the screens, and you're having a cup of coffee and I'm having a cup of tea, and our feet are touching under the covers.'

Joshua shook his head. He turned around. After a while he came and sat down next to me. Already I felt like – a dead tree that someone kept hacking at with an axe.

'Natalie, listen,' he said.

22

A lone violin played. Its ragged keening was squeezed through two small speakers.

'A Life in Literature'

the screen announced. And then I watched as tea-coloured lithographs slowly dissolved into misty photographs, ragged-edged portraiture. A horse and covered wagon at a junction became a line of ladies in bonnets. A moustachioed man, sitting stiffly in an armchair, faded into a boy with dark eyes. The narrator had a low, patrician voice. He told gravely of Thomas Wolfe's harried upbringing, with his mother the speculator and his father a rambunctious tombstone maker. When Wolfe left Asheville for Chapel Hill University, the soundtrack changed: to honky-tonk piano. The noble intonations persisted.

The original 'Dixieland' boarding house, the Old Kentucky Home, had nearly burned down, and was still being restored. On the front of the fundraising leaflet for that was a bright photo of the building as it had been, painted lemon yellow, with a grand white veranda. I remembered reading in *The Lost Summer*, about Mrs Wolfe chasing Fitzgerald away from there when he went for a look-see, hectoring him down the steps with: 'I never take drunks – not if I know it.'

This high-altitude city, 'The Land in the Sky', with its sunny arcades and its undulating horizons, what a place for a spree, after all.

In the temporary visitor's centre there were only a few strange artefacts to squint at, point out, make some vague and earnest attempt to 'take in'. When Wolfe described going back home, running a hand along the old banister, he wrote, '*This was Time.*'

This is Time, I thought.

Joshua had already wandered on through to the small gift shop, and soon I followed him.

'*You Can't Go Home Again,*' he said. 'Did you read this?'

'I did, when I knew I was coming here.'

'Yeah, I guess I started to read it once.'

'I bought it second-hand,' I said. 'On the flyleaf someone had written, "Wolfe was Right, By God!" And then all the way through, there were these wobbling underlinings in the same green ink. Arbitrarily deployed, but relentless, on every page, like the blips on a heart monitor. It was – irritating.'

Joshua was standing with one shoulder leant against the wall, flicking through the copy he was holding. He looked good today. He'd had a shave and slicked his straggly hair down. The bone-white side parting bowed over his ear. Instead of his cardigan he was wearing a grey check sports coat, slightly too short in the sleeve. It still had grass cuttings pressed on its back, from when we had a roll around at lunchtime. He'd kept grabbing my behind then. He'd said, 'There's gold in them there hills.'

'Vigour is the word they always use, but it's true,' I said, touching the top of the book. 'Writing like that is a strange physical feat. It overwhelmed me a little. He was being absolutely sincere.'

From the display rack I picked up a book called *Thomas Wolfe: Three Decades of Criticism*.

'I like this,' I said. 'It's amusing to me.'

'How's that?'

'I don't know,' I said. Then, '*Joshua Spassky: Thirty-three Years of Gripes.*'

Joshua shook his head.

I said, 'You know, I think I've developed one

of those dismal senses of humour that depressed people get – flippant and fatuous.'

He closed the book.

'You worry too much,' he said, and then, 'I guess I'll buy this. Seems like – a good memento.'

'Does it?' I said. 'Well, let me get it, then. I can write some kind of pertinent dedication.'

He waited outside while I went to the till. I could see him standing by the wooden gate, hands in his pockets and his head tilted to the right. He leant on one foot and then the other, then he stretched his arms in front of him, and shook his head as though he was clearing it. Finally he sat down on the kerb and rested his hands on his knees. Tall, clumpy trees stood either side of him. His jacket was stretched over his back, and his slicked hair was curling up again.

I leant on the balustrade to write in his book, circling my pen over the first blank page.

'I like your outfit today, Joshua,' I said, as I walked down the gravel path towards him. 'You look like James Bond.'

He took my hand but he didn't stand up; he pulled me down to sit next to him, instead. I kept hold of his warm hand, pressed it against my face, pressed down on his pebbly knuckles.

He smelt of the soap in the hotel bathroom; the pearly-pink liquid in the bottle on the cistern.

I went on: 'Yesterday you looked like Christ after he'd been taken down from the cross. Or maybe Ben Gunn, or Oblomov.'

'Ya. I was pretty sick,' he said, and he nodded to himself. He turned to me and smiled.

I didn't say it, but I thought it so strongly it was as good as saying it. I saw him understand me. I thought, Oh, I've done it now.

We sat in silence for a while. And then Joshua nudged me and pointed across the street.

'You see that,' he said, 'that apartment.'

I looked where he was looking, up at the large windows over a candle shop. The bamboo blinds were rolled up there, and inside was a large, light living room. I could just see the top of a bald head poking over the top of an elephant-cord sofa, also a full bookcase, and an ugly abstract painting – a stringy net of egg yellow punctuated with scabs of blue-black – hanging over a crowded mantelpiece.

'That could be my place,' Joshua said. 'Back home. Where I live is this studio on the second floor, just catty-corner to a cafeteria, and basically anyone passing can see right in. If you stand opposite, and up on tiptoe, you can see the whole place. There's no hiding. If I want to lay low, you know? I have to literally do that – lie on the floor like a kid. If I sit at my desk, they can see me. They can see who's in there with me, too, which can be a problem. I can draw the curtains, but then there'll be a light on . . . It's kind of ridiculous. And on top of that, there's the fact that, like, my car is parked outside. People get so mad if you don't answer the phone, don't they? They really get mad.'

'Do they?' I said.

We stopped looking up at the flat, then.

'When people want you to come out it's kind of rude not to,' he said. 'Isn't it?'

'I don't know,' I said. 'After I stopped drinking, when people phoned up, I'd see their names flashing on the screen and I couldn't answer, because the fact was, there wasn't any line of communication from where I was to – anywhere else. It was like they were calling from the very bottom of the memory hole. I took one step back from life, and then another step back. And that was all it took.'

Joshua shrugged. I put my hand on the back of his head, felt his sun-warmed hair.

'Are we going to go get a drink now?' he said. 'Is it that time?'

'It probably is,' I said.

We stood up together, and started walking along the road, our hands held, no tighter, no looser than usual, just hanging there between us.

'So, are you still living in that same place?' Joshua said.

I shook my head.

'No,' I said. 'Not any more.'

We kept on, uphill towards the corner of College Street and Broadway. We were silent for a while, and then Joshua said, 'So I guess the worst thing I've ever heard, was last summer . . . There was this girl I was dating, and we went out to the park one Sunday, me, her and her Mom, kind of for a picnic?'

He was looking across at me, so I nodded.

'It was this whole – I don't know. We were drinking white wine and we had these salads in – tubs. Anyway. At some point, her mother said, "So, Joshua, tell me about yourself."'

We'd stopped at the junction now, halfway across the road, and I'd turned about to face him.

'I was saying to this girl afterwards,' he said, 'I felt like standing up and leaving right then.'

He rubbed one eye. He kept looking at me, or at least, squinting at whatever he could see;

that sun was still behind me, I was probably just a grey shape, a dark nub in the starchy brightness. It had been the other way around earlier, when we were lying down on the grass; I'd had to shield my eyes with the crook of my arm, his face was so vague and washed out, against the spikes of light radiating from under one ear.

But there was a car coming up the hill. I heard it and looked back. It was an old, red Ford, bumping slowly towards us, as if it were being lazily winched. I stepped out of its way, took Joshua's hand again, and we both stepped up onto the pavement.

'I'm just picturing you,' I said, 'crouching on tartan, perturbed, with a half-eaten chicken leg.'

'Yeah. I just, I didn't really answer the question,' he said.

23

Now the book was on a wobbly little café table, along with his glass of orange juice, and my glass of fizzing tonic water. A folded serviette fluttered under each drink. An oxbow of coloured light lay long on the white marble.

This was the only unshaded place on the terrace. The other tables looked chilly; people were putting their jackets and cardigans on again. The hairs were standing up on my arms, too. I rubbed my forearms and tried to warm up.

'So, I've been thinking about booking a plane ticket home,' Joshua said.

I looked up, nodded once.

'I don't want to sit on that bus again,' he said. 'There's an airport here, right? You flew in?'

'I did, yes. The airport is maybe fifteen, twenty minutes away.'

'I guess I should sort that out. We only have one day left, right? Is that right?'

I nodded again. 'Mmhmm. Well, it's today.'

'Because that bus was really bad,' he said. 'You know. It smelt of – hair grease.'

He smiled, rubbed a hand over one eye.

'Oh,' he said, 'I meant to ask you this, too, incidentally. On like, the first leg of the journey, there was a woman on the row behind me who kept complaining about the heat, and saying that she had lupus and she needed to be cool. Do you know what lupus is?'

I shook my head.

'No, I've never heard of it.'

'Well, me neither, but obviously it sounds like lupine, so I thought werewolves, right? And then I thought maybe she just had excess body hair, and so for the next three hours I was really wanting to turn around and look, because I was picturing this bearded lady, you know, fanning herself with *People* magazine? But then when she got off the bus, she was just, you know, not hairy at all, so . . . Anyway. I wondered if you knew.'

I shook my head.

'Are you flying back to Manchester?' he said.

I took hold of the thick edge of the tabletop and looked around the bright street; I tapped one foot on the ground.

'Are you okay?' Joshua said.

I scratched on my forehead before I answered.

'I'm fine,' I said.

Across the road, a young woman was pulling rolled-up posters from her messenger bag and standing on a chair to stick them up in the window of the bookshop. That building was painted mauve; the ceramics shop next to it was a fresh, lime green. All the windows of all these places were bright with these photocopied announcements.

'I've been meaning to tell you this, too,' Joshua went on, 'that I had a pretty awkward phone call yesterday, you know, while you were out.'

'Oh right,' I said.

'Well, it was just this – it was Connie, you know, I mentioned her. She's, understandably, not too happy that I'm down here with this – girl from Europe.'

'Oh, is she not?' I said.

He widened his eyes and shook his head slowly.

I picked up my drink and looked down into it, shook the lumps of ice about so the bubbles came up quicker.

When I looked at him again, Joshua had his head tilted to one side, one hand squeezing the back of his neck.

I put my glass back down.

'I don't know what to say,' I said.

Before I'd finished speaking he'd shrugged again, twitched his shoulders.

'I'm not asking you to say anything.'

'Okay,' I said. 'Well, that's alright then.'

Joshua looked down, He ran his tongue around under his lips.

The silence wasn't even uncomfortable: Joshua pushing his drink around the table, me snapping toothpicks. But anyway, after a while, I stood up, scraped my chair back.

'I'm getting another drink,' I said. 'Do you want one?'

'No,' Joshua said, looking up at me, smiling amiably. 'No, I'm good.'

With my eyes used to the sun, the tenebrous indoors was hard to navigate. I stopped just past the doorway and blinked hard a few times. I shook my head to clear it. All this drama.

At the bar I asked for a tonic water, and downed it where I stood. The barman leant back against the fridges, next to the payphone.

He was wiping his hands on a green Coor's towel. When the phone started ringing he answered it immediately, then turned away, bowed his head, and started giggling down the line.

Through the narrow row of windows, I could still see Joshua. A boy wandering by stopped and handed him a flyer. Joshua took the coloured piece of paper and folded it up without looking at it, put it under the book. Again he picked up his drink and sat back, tucked a fallen lick of hair behind his ear. I did wonder about him. He'd come all this way. He was sitting out there with an orange juice, rolling the glass along his forehead, now, closing his eyes.

I paid for another drink and took it out with me, put it on the table. I didn't sit down, though, I just stood behind my chair, leant on its iron back, heavily, so the front legs lifted up, an inch or so off the concrete. I turned on the spot and leant down on the chair back.

'What you were saying before,' I said, 'I've been going over it and I think it could make a good basis for a short film.'

'What's that?' Joshua said. 'What was I saying?'

'Just before, walking up. A good title for a certain kind of independent film would be *Now Tell Me Something About You*. Don't you think?'

I went on. 'The opening shot could be: a girl in her pyjamas, still half asleep, sitting at her kitchen table. The camera's facing her, straight on. The flat she's in is scruffy looking, too. Maybe it has a pitched roof. Anyway, what's noticeable is that she has a big rotary telephone on the table next to her, and also a full in-tray, maybe even a rolodex. She's got her coffee mug in one hand, and probably it's one of those oversize hippy mugs – with a cat painted on it or something, I don't know. In the other hand she has a pen, a Biro, and she's tapping it on the table as she stares straight ahead and blinks sleepily. Then her gaze becomes more focused on the viewer, and more focused still, and a quaint, cold smile plays across her lips; she lifts her chin and draws breath to speak . . . and then we cut to – the title card: Now Tell Me Something About You.'

Joshua had screwed up one eye.

'That's as far as I've got,' I said.

'Natalie, you have to calm down.'

'Do I? Okay.'

Another silence, and I set the chair I was leaning on down again.

But all I'd ever had to go on were these impulses.

24

Joshua was looking down at his hands. On the table were the book and the half-drunk drinks. That faint pluck of sunlight still disclosed our fingerprints on the glasses.

I looked around at the other tables, mostly empty now. I said, 'I wondered if I was coming out here to say goodbye.'

Joshua looked up.

'Oh,' he said. 'Goodbye. Really?'

'I wondered.'

'Well,' he said, 'I don't know about that. Goodbye. That's kind of rude, isn't it?'

'I don't know,' I said.

25

I was breathing very deeply, blinking wetly. There was a slight deafness. And a bright light. No, I couldn't go on.

'Natalie? What's the matter? Natalie? Look at me, come on. It's okay.'

I didn't look though. We fell back awkwardly, still in a heavy clinch, and I kept my face turned away. I wiped at my eyes with my free hand.

'I'm sorry,' I said.

'Don't be sorry.'

'I am sorry.'

I was facing the front wall. Joshua had pulled the curtain cord as soon as we'd got in and I'd watched those heavy green drapes jerk towards each other. Now I held onto him. His slick back. It took a few more minutes. When we looked at each other again, he raised his eyebrows and then I raised my eyebrows, too. I shook my head.

It was a while before he spoke. He frowned and then he said, 'You know, I think I actually prefer the crying, to the sex.'

'Oh no.'

'But I do.'

'Don't say that.'

'But I do.'

'Oh dear,' I said. 'I'll have to think about this.'

Joshua touched my feet with his foot. There was the smooth hard skin on the bottom of his big toe. I was lying on my side and looking at him. He was still rubbing my back.

'Did I ever tell you,' he said, 'that I cried when I first saw *ET*? A couple of my brothers took me, and I remember sitting in the theatre, absolutely straight up in my seat, trying to keep my eyes wide open. I didn't dare blink. But they spotted it: "Are you *crying*, Joshy?" I was so worried they were going to tell people at school. They didn't though. So. It was okay.'

He was lying there, blinking back at me. There was his broad face, his beard coming through again; thick filaments, some amber, some black, were sprouting on his cheeks and on the dip under his bottom lip. I reached up and gave his face a scratch. He closed his eyes and tilted his chin back. The last of the daylight was ebbing away now, and the room was getting cooler.

'Anyways,' Joshua said. 'Why me? You know.'

'Why you what?'

He shrugged at me.

'Well, you're a nice-looking young woman,' he said, 'Well turned out. I like your work.'

I shook my head.

After a moment we both shifted up the bed, and sat against the headboard, both with our legs drawn up and crossed. He put his arm around me and I held his hand.

'I guess when you meet someone new you always think they're going to be the answer to all of your problems,' he said. 'Right?'

Again I shook my head. I looked at his hand in mine.

'Well. No,' I said. 'No. I can't say I've ever felt like that. Nobody's going to say anything life-saving to you, are they? When you hold another person, I think you're only ever really holding onto your own fathomless situation. But maybe that's why –'

Joshua rubbed his free hand over his face.

'Christ, you sound like me,' he said. He sighed very deeply then and he looked over at me.

'So do you think you and I are maybe just – I don't know – do you think we're just self-pity times two?' he said. 'And is another body really any use in that case? I mean, I don't know. I'm asking the question. What do you think?'

'What do I think?' I said. 'Well, I don't think I do feel self-pity exactly. I think I was crying because . . .'

Joshua was looking at me and I had to look away. My heart was beating unpleasantly. I said, 'I think we're just, you know . . . I think we really are . . .'

I stood up, tugged one of the scratchy yellow blankets off the bed and wrapped it around myself.

Joshua's hands were around his knees. He squinted across at me.

'I remember when I very first saw you,' he said. 'I saw you come into the bar and I thought, Oh God, another pretty girl. This is exactly what I don't need.'

He chewed at a fingernail for a second, and then he pointed at me with that finger.

'That's great, Joshua,' I said. 'I'm going to have a bath now. I feel funny.'

I sat up in the warm water for a while. The hazy water moved around me and the soap-film on the surface caught the lack of light. When I slid back and put my head under, beneath the turbine rumble of the fan, I could still make out Joshua's low tones, on the phone to somebody out there.

I turned the dull metal latch to let the water out, and as it was pulled slowly away, the blue razor handle bobbed around the island of my right knee. I stood up then and turned the misted dial as far left as it would go, moved the other switch to 'Shower'. It wasn't uncomfortable to begin with. I lifted my arms up, turned the dial until the water was blasting out. I rinsed my hair and threw handfuls of cold water up over my face.

Of course I'd left long before I took that train out of Manchester. And leaving had felt like snipping myself out of a thick skein. I'd been aware of that sensation particularly: cords fraying and snapping.

At the edges of the small mirror, drips fell over fingerprints that swarmed like bacilli. There I was again. In a wiped-out porthole. I pushed my wet hair back, lifted my chin up.

Joshua was sitting on the edge of the bed. He'd put his shirt back on. I went and sat up next to him. The windows were open behind the curtains and a breeze was making them softly swell. After a moment he said, 'So you really think we're in love then?'

'I do,' I said.

He nodded once.

'Okay. Well, that's good. Right? I mean, I think we're in love too, so –'

'So –'

Soon we both lay down.

Joshua was holding onto me. I felt his hands squeeze my waist.

'You're cold,' he said.

'Yes,' I said, 'I feel like – a milk bottle that's just been taken out of the fridge.'

I stroked the back of his head. I laughed to myself without meaning to. I said, 'And you're like – a stray tomcat who's just sneaked into the kitchen.'

Joshua frowned at me.

'Natalie, you don't need to talk like that anymore,' he said.

And so I never did.

penguin.co.uk/vintage